KUMA KUMA KUMA BEAR

CONTENTS

KUMA KUMA KUMA BEAR

NOVEL

WRITTEN BY
Kumanano

ILLUSTRATED BY
029

Airship

Seven Seas Entertainment

KUMA KUMA KUMA BEAR Vol. 7
© KUMANANO 2017

Illustrated by 029

Originally published in Japan in 2017 by
SHUFU TO SEIKATSU SHA CO., LTD., Tokyo.
English translation rights arranged with
SHUFU TO SEIKATSU SHA CO., LTD., Tokyo,
through TOHAN CORPORATION, Tokyo.

Seven Seas press and purchase enquiries can be sent to
Marketing Manager Lianne Sentar at press@gomanga.com.
Information regarding the distribution and purchase of
digital editions is available from Digital Manager CK Russell
at digital@gomanga.com.

Seven Seas and the Seven Seas logo are trademarks of
Seven Seas Entertainment. All rights reserved.

Follow Seven Seas Entertainment online at
sevenseasentertainment.com.

TRANSLATION: Jan Cash & Vincent Castaneda
COVER DESIGN: Kris Aubin
INTERIOR DESIGN: Clay Gardner
INTERIOR LAYOUT: George Panella
PROOFREADER: Meg van Huygen, Stephanie Cohen
LIGHT NOVEL EDITOR: Nibedita Sen
PREPRESS TECHNICIAN: Rhiannon Rasmussen-Silverstein
PRODUCTION MANAGER: Lissa Pattillo
MANAGING EDITOR: Julie Davis
ASSOCIATE PUBLISHER: Adam Arnold
PUBLISHER: Jason DeAngelis

ISBN: 978-1-64827-239-4
Printed in Canada
First Printing: August 2021
10 9 8 7 6 5 4 3 2 1

Skills

▶ FANTASY WORLD LANGUAGE
The fantasy world's language will sound like Japanese.
Spoken words are conveyed to the other party in the fantasy world language.

▶ FANTASY WORLD LITERACY
The ability to read the fantasy world writing.
Written words become the fantasy world's words.

▶ BEAR EXTRADIMENSIONAL STORAGE
The white bear's mouth opens into infinite space. It can hold (eat) anything.
However, it cannot hold (eat) living things.
Time will stop for objects that are inside of it.
Anything that is put into the extradimensional storage can be pulled out at any time.

▶ BEAR IDENTIFICATION
By looking through the bear eyes on the Bear Clothes' hood, one can see the effects of a weapon or tool.
Doesn't work without wearing the hood.

▶ BEAR DETECTION
Using the wild abilities of bears, can detect monsters or people.

▶ BEAR MAP 2.0
Any area looked at by the bear eyes can be made into a map.

▶ BEAR SUMMONING
Bears can be summoned from the bear gloves.
A black bear can be summoned from the black glove.
A white bear can be summoned from the white glove.

▶ BEAR TRANSPORTER GATE
By setting up a gate, can move between gates.
When more than three gates are in place, can travel to a location by picturing it.
This gate can only be opened with the bear hand.

▶ BEAR PHONE
Can have long-distance conversations with others.
Phone persists until caster dispels it. Physically indestructible.
Can call people a bear phone is given to by picturing the person.
Incoming call is announced by the sound of a bear's cry.

Magic

▶ BEAR LIGHT
Mana collected in the bear glove creates a light in the shape of a bear.

▶ BEAR PHYSICAL ENHANCEMENT
Routing mana through the bear gear allows for physical enhancement.

▶ BEAR FIRE MAGIC
Based on the mana that is gathered in the bear glove, gives the ability to use fire elemental magic.
Power is proportional to mana and the mental image.
When imagining a bear, power increases even more.

▶ BEAR WATER MAGIC
Based on the mana that is gathered in the bear glove, gives the ability to use water elemental magic.
Power is proportional to mana and the mental image.
When imagining a bear, power increases even more.

▶ BEAR WIND MAGIC
Based on the mana that is gathered in the bear glove, gives the ability to use wind elemental magic.
Power is proportional to mana and the mental image.
When imagining a bear, power increases even more.

▶ BEAR EARTH MAGIC
Based on the mana that is gathered in the bear glove, gives the ability to use earth elemental magic.
Power is proportional to mana and the mental image.
When imagining a bear, power increases even more.

▶ BEAR HEALING MAGIC
Can give treatment by means of the bear's kind heart.

🐻 Equipment

▶ **BLACK BEAR GLOVE (NONTRANSFERABLE)**
Attack glove, increases power based on the user's level.

▶ **WHITE BEAR GLOVE (NONTRANSFERABLE)**
Defense glove, increases defense based on the user's level.

▶ **BLACK BEAR SHOE (NONTRANSFERABLE)**

▶ **WHITE BEAR SHOE (NONTRANSFERABLE)**
Increases speed based on the user's level.
Prevents fatigue when walking long distances based on the user's level.

▶ **BLACK AND WHITE BEAR CLOTHES (NONTRANSFERABLE)**
Appears to be a onesie. Reversible.
FRONT: BLACK BEAR CLOTHES
Increases physical and magic resistance based on the user's level.
Gives heat and cold resistance.
REVERSE: WHITE BEAR CLOTHES
Automatically restores health and mana while worn.
Amount and speed based on the user's level.
Gives heat and cold resistance.

▶ **BEAR UNDERWEAR (NONTRANSFERABLE)**
Won't get dirty no matter how much they're used.
An excellent item that won't retain sweat or smells.
Will grow with the user.

KUMA
KUMA
KUMA
BEAR

KUMA
KUMA
KUMA
BEAR

149

The Bear Goes to the Mines
(The Hero Goes to the Mines)

ONCE UPON A TIME, a princess, Fina, was taken captive by a terrible witch, Ellelaura. The witch would likely gift Princess Fina a beautiful room, dress her in extravagant clothes, and grant her a soft bed. She would likely also present Princess Fina all kinds of tasty treats to undermine her resolve (and give her a tummy ache).

Until the hero—that's Yuna—returned, Princess Fina would be forced to tour the royal capital and hang out with Ellelaura's daughter, Shia. Princess Fina would doubtless be weeping (with joy, admittedly).

Only by slaying the golem in the terrible witch's mines could Princess Fina escape.

"Oh, Princess Fina, please wait for me," proclaimed the hero, Yuna, to the captive princess. "For I shall surely defeat the golem and return to you."

She had to rescue the princess quickly—she vowed in her heart she would. And so the hero turned her back on the witch's abode and began her journey.

...All right, fine. In real life, I spent the night hanging out with Fina at Ellelaura's house, then left the next morning.

The Adventurer Guild master, Sanya, had told me that the fastest route to the mines was from the capital. Once I was outside the capital, I summoned Kumayuru and we headed for the mine.

After some breaks and a switch over to Kumakyu, I caught sight of a small town. Most of the people living there were involved with the mines—they were people who sought ore and the merchants who did business with the miners. Eventually, shops had sprung up around them, then houses, and before you knew it, a tiny town had emerged here.

I got off of Kumakyu and headed the rest of the way on foot, so I wouldn't cause a commotion in town with my huge magical bear.

When I made it into town, I attracted the usual attention.

I pulled my bear hood low over my face to hide and tried not to pay it too much mind while I looked for an inn.

Still, the town wasn't exactly what you'd call lively. It gave me real "Mileela beseiged by that kraken" vibes, which...I guess made sense, on account of those golems in the mines. Maybe I could learn more about that at the inn.

While I was walking along and planning, somebody called for me from behind, "Is that you, Yuna?!"

And who should show up but Jaden and Mel, those two I'd met while guarding the students, accompanied by a man and woman. I knew Jaden and Mel from when I'd seen them during the guarding quest the other day, but even though I should have known the other two from the Adventurer Guild, they hadn't made an impression in my memory. All I remembered was their gender.

"I knew it, it *was* Yuna," Mel declared giddily.

"Anyone would know that just by looking," a woman in her twenties said with a deadpan sigh.

"Ah, been a while, hasn't it, bear girl?" the other guy greeted me. He seemed the youngest out of all of them. Even though he was saying it had been a while, I couldn't remember when the last while was. I've got to have plenty of room in my brain for more important stuff.

"What are you doing here, Yuna?" asked Jaden.

"Well, basically for a job."

He tilted his head. "You're not here to slay the golems too, are you?"

"Based on that 'too,' I take it you took the quest as well?" Made sense. I guess these were the C-Rank adventurers I'd heard about.

"Yeah, we've been slaying golems for a few days now. We just came back from the tunnels, matter of fact."

"How's it going? If you're basically done, then I'll just head home," I asked, trying not to sound as hopeful as I felt. That'd make things so much easier...

"It's not over yet."

"It's not?" Ugh, was the quest really difficult enough that it was giving C-Rank adventurers a hard time?

Since we'd stopped right in the middle of the road to talk, Mel broke in on the conversation. "Jaden, we shouldn't have a whole conversation out here. How about we talk about it over dinner at the inn?"

I looked around. We *were* getting some looks. Jaden's party of eye-catching adventurers was already enough to draw attention, and here was a girl in a bear onesie. It'd be weird if we *didn't* stand out. (Although most of the stares were probably for me, anyway.)

"Right, guess we're due for a change of scenery."

Yeah, I was all for that...and I wanted to get a room as

soon as I could. If there weren't any available, I'd have to set up my traveling bear house.

We headed toward the inn where Jaden's party was staying, introducing one another as we went. The swordsman guy was Toya. He gave off this kind of chill-but-fickle vibe. The woman in light clothes with the deadpan tone was named Senia. I guess she was what you'd call a frigid beauty.

Jaden's party led me to the inn. Once we settled down, I'd need to gather info about where the mines were... but wait, *where* would I do that? Did this town have an adventurers' guild? Guess I'd need to ask around.

When Jaden headed inside the lobby, the woman behind the counter called out to him. "Welcome back, Jaden. Came back in one piece for another day then?"

"We did."

"Well, then, how was it?" she asked, and Jaden just shook his head. "That bad, huh? But you made a new friend? That young girl behind you, dressed as a bear..."

"Oh, that's Yuna. She's a full-fledged adventurer, believe it or not. Seems she came to slay the golems that appeared in the mines too," Jaden answered with a grin.

"Her? An adventurer?!"

Another phenomenal introduction for the bear girl. Not that I could blame them, considering how rare-to-mostly-nonexistent us bear adventurers probably were.

"She's too cute," the proprietress said dubiously. "No one that cute could be an adventurer."

"No, we can all vouch for her abilities. Also, she needs a room—do you have one open?"

"If *you're* vouching for her, Jaden, then it must be true. And yes, I do have one room."

Good. I wouldn't have to set up my bear house on the outskirts of town.

"Aww, too bad," said Mel. "If you didn't have any vacancies, I was thinking she could stay with us."

"Our rooms are doubles," Senia snapped.

"Oh, c'mon, it'd work out. See, I'd sleep next to Yuna, and she'd fit just fine. I mean, if she took off that bulky bear costume, ya know?"

Uh. Yikes. No way was I doing *that*. It was one thing in the safety of my own home, but I wasn't taking off my bear gear in this place where who-knows-what could happen. Plus, if I did that, I wouldn't be able to summon my guards, Kumayuru and Kumakyu.

Once I got myself a room, we decided to continue our earlier conversation over dinner.

"All right, so what's the situation with the golems?"

"To summarize it...we've got no clue."

"No matter how many times we destroy the golems, they just respawn after a while. There never seem to be more than a set number, but almost all of them are back by the next day."

Was it an infinite spawn point? Any gamer would be thrilled to hear about that. You could get tons of experience and money depending on the types of item drops. Deep within my gamer heart, I still felt a pang of joy at the thought ...

"We think it has something to do with a golem the miners spotted deep in the mines."

According to Jaden, the miners had unearthed a giant cavern during their excavations. There'd been a golem right in the center of the place, and the miners had run off when the golem came to life. After that, more golems showed up—a *lot* more golems.

Hmm...that chamber they'd found the golem in seemed mighty suspicious. Maybe it had a golem-making thingamajig or something?

"You haven't tried going to slay that first golem?" That seemed like the best thing to do, right? If it failed, back to the drawing board, but they *had* to start with that one before moving onto the next theory.

"It's not that simple. The deeper you go into the mines, the stronger the golems get."

"As in multiple golems, right?"

"You already knew about those?"

"I heard that's why the quest wound up getting bumped all the way to Rank C...and even you guys are having trouble, yeah?"

"Right. The problem isn't whether we can slay them— it's that they're a gigantic pain."

Oh, I bet they were. When you were in a confined space, you were limited when it came to offensive measures. Hulking iron golems in tiny passageways would be *rough.* "But you *can* defeat them, right? Couldn't you just keep pushing forward?"

"Well...see, there's this huge cavern you hit before you reach the room they found that golem, see? In that cavern, you've got five whole iron golems in there. One or two...we can deal with that. Five is trouble."

So basically, they couldn't go deeper in because of those golems. Hmm. Iron golems, huh? Was there a way to get rid of them without making the tunnels collapse?

Jaden's party went on to tell me a few more things, some of them news to me.

"Are you sure you should be telling me this stuff? Isn't it normal to keep info like this to yourself?"

If another party on the same quest beats you to the punch, you lose the reward. Basically, Jaden and I were competing for the same thing.

"No, this is an emergency. If we had more time to burn, we could've tried out more options, but the guild is pressuring us to get it done quick. More firepower's what we need—even if we can only get a little more of it. Besides, at this rate, we'll end up failing the quest. That'd be a real bad problem for us."

"Would you get credit for the quest if I were the one doing the slaying?"

"Credit for the kill always goes to the slayer, but that wouldn't mark the quest as a failure. It'd be treated as a joint guest and we'd get a small reward. We just gotta contribute to the work. Anyway, we've already made a killing selling off iron golem parts, so I don't mind telling you this stuff."

Mel nodded. "Actually, it'd *help* us if you slay them."

Looked like it didn't matter if I was the slayer. In that case, I didn't have to worry about Jaden's party—I could just get rid of those golems.

"Thanks for sharing so much of your intel with me. That's helped a ton."

If I'd tried to gather that info alone, it wouldn't have nearly been this simple. They'd saved me a ton of time.

Princess Fina...wait for me!

We'd finished eating, but there was a commotion at the entrance before I could head to my room. Unfamiliar voices.

"Whew, I'm beat."

"Yeah, seriously. Just one iron golem after another."

"Ehh, at least we made some scratch off 'em."

"Good ol' golems, heh."

"Anyway, let's get something to eat fast. I'm starving."

Five adventurers had entered and, at first glance, they did *not* look like anybody I wanted to be involved with. (Look, it takes one to know one.)

What was *with* these getups?

The man at the front had bright red hair and the armor to match. If there'd been any bulls around, this guy would've been mata-*gored*.

The second person was dressed in...blue armor? The third one, green. The fourth was a mage wearing a black mantle. Finally there was a lone woman (the only one?) in her thirties wearing a white mantle. This was one vivid group of five.

If they'd only been dressed in yellow and pink instead of white and black, they would've looked like some pretty powerful rangers. Then again...though yellow clothes were doable if gaudy in this world, a pink mantle was right out.

The colorful squad of five came by.

The red guy looked at me and snorted. "Yo, Jaden. Since when did you jerk-offs get a pet bear?"

The other four behind him laughed. Well, then, I dub thee the bozo rangers.

"She's an adventurer, you know. Also, she's in Rank C, same as us."

"You kidding me? That bear's an adventurer? Quit pullin' my leg."

Wow. He wasn't even going after my rank first—he was questioning whether I could even *be* an adventurer, which...actually made a lot of sense, now that I thought about it. Hm.

"And besides, Rank C? If you're going to make jokes, at least make 'em funny."

Bozo Red guffawed. "Nahh, I guess she's funny enough just by existing, eh? Well, enough about the bear. How'd today go? We took out three iron golems. Couldn't be better."

No, *not* enough with the bear. This guy called me a pet. The duel was on.

But they ignored my seething rage and kept the conversation going.

"We got three too."

"You did? Guess you losers are pulling your weight. Of course, you're gonna let *us* handle those five golems deep in the mines. Once we slay that golem in the back, this quest is in the bag."

Bozo Ranger Red left, cackling all the while. The storm was over, and silence was all that remained.

Okay, so...the bozo rangers also thought that golem in the back of the mines was suspect.

"That guy's name was Barbould," said Jaden. "They're adventurers like us who came here for the golem quest. They're in Rank C and they've got awful personalities, but they're not bad people. They also pack a punch in battle."

Yeah, Sanya *had* told me there were two parties here. I disagreed on the "they're not bad people" part, but they had to be decent fighters at the very least if they could slay iron golems.

"Still, I can't believe they'd call Yuna a pet," Mel said. "They're obviously wrong—she's a *mascot*."

No, you're *wrong. I'm not a pet or mascot,* I retorted mentally.

"Judging from what Barbould said, golems seem to go for a pretty good price."

"Seems like it."

Golems were considered monsters too, so the parts belonged to the adventurer who defeated them. They would go for a pretty penny, now that I thought about it. "You haven't sold the ones you got, Jaden?" I asked. "You just mentioned you took down three of them."

"We sell them the legitimate way, so they don't sell for as much. We're still getting 20 percent more than what they usually go for, though."

Mel sighed. "I heard that those guys get 50 percent more."

I didn't know how much they sold for wholesale, but that seemed pretty profitable. Unlike in the game, the golems wouldn't disappear when you beat them, so you could trade the whole carcass in.

KUMA
KUMA
KUMA
BEAR

150

The Bear Enters the Mines
Part One

TODAY, ON BEARQUEST...

To rescue the hostage Princess Fina from the terrible witch Ellelaura, the great Hero, Yuna, has arrived at the mines, but...

Hark! A golem blocks heroic Yuna's way! The golem extends its arm and launches a never-ending barrage of pebbles at her. Our hero dodges, but...can she avoid them all? Alas, nope.

Fwunk fwunk, fwunk fwunk.

The rocks pebble her cheeks, but they do not hurt. They feel soft. Such lame attacks cannot defeat mighty Yuna!

The hero runs at the golem. To keep her at bay, the golem pelts her with a deluge of rocks.

Fwunk fwunk, fwunk fwunk.

Pah! 'Tis nothing. The Hero Yuna laughs at such weak attacks.

Fwunk fwunk, fwunk fwunk.

As Yuna ignores the assailing rocks, she raises her mighty sword for a stab...and does not feel the sword connect! Thwarted, heroic Yuna tries to use magic, but instead, she abruptly feels as though she is being suffocated.

Was this, too, an attack?!

Something...presses...against...her face...

Oxygen...fading...

Heroic Yuna is defenseless against this mysterious assault. Would she die without even knowing what killed her?

And so our hero falls into the abyss of unconsciousness...

"Ahh! Can't breathe."

Thud.

I got up and something slipped off my face.

"Kumakyu?"

Kumakyu looked quizzically at me, lying right in front of my eyes. Kumayuru sat curled up on top of my belly. I didn't leave myself defenseless, after all, even while asleep—I'd summoned my bears in cub form as a preventative measure.

"I'm gonna blame that dream on you guys, you know." Those soft *fwunk*s must've been their paws, and I'd been suffocating because Kumakyu had been smothering me in my sleep. "What was up with that?"

Kumayuru and Kumakyu gave a little "Kwoom" in reply and looked toward the window.

The sun was streaming in. Apparently, they'd just tried to wake me up, since it was morning. I guess I *had* asked them to wake me up before we went to bed, but...

"I love you guys, but can you not smother me to wake me up next time?"

I'd been *this* close to suffocating to death. If I'd been just a little too late waking up, I would've ended up in the obituaries. "Onesie Girl Found Dead." Ack, what a thought.

Still, Kumayuru and Kumakyu had kept me from sleeping in. I had to be grateful. It wouldn't be right to *bear* a grudge against them.

I thanked Kumayuru and Kumakyu, then sent them back. I also changed from my white bear outfit to my black one and headed to the dining room for breakfast.

While I was eating alone, Mel and Senia came by. I didn't see Jaden or Toya.

"Good morning, Yuna," said Mel. Senia gave me a casual wave.

"Mel, Senia. Good morning."

"Are you going to the mines soon?" he asked.

"I was thinking of going to check it out at least." I mean, I had to get through this quest quick so I could save Princess Fina.

"In that case, you want to head in with us?"

"You mean your party? Today?"

"We know you can hold your own," said Mel, "but you really don't look like it."

Senia nodded. "I really can't see you as any more than a cute bear."

And they began patting my head. Really? *Really?*

"You don't look like you're all that strong. We're worried," said Mel.

"That's why Mel and I spoke about it yesterday," said Senia.

I got that they were concerned about me, but it was easier to do things on my own. Then again, I still kind of wanted to see their abilities in action.

Hmm. What did I want more?

I guess the answer to *that* was for them to stop patting me on the head...and right when I thought that, they stopped, sat down next to me, and ordered breakfast.

"But shouldn't you ask Jaden whether he's okay with that?" I asked.

"We don't need to ask him," Mel declared.

Wait up, wasn't Jaden the leader? They couldn't just do stuff like that without at least consulting him. While the bloc of women in the group discussed that with each other, Jaden and the other guy came down from the second floor.

"You're all early."

"You're all just slow. Oh, and Yuna is coming with us to go investigate the mines."

Hey, wait a minute, I still hadn't said anything yet. When did that get decided?!

"Yeah, all right."

"Fine by me too."

They were agreeing just like that? No discussion or anything? Well, nobody heard my internal pleas. In the end, I was swept up by the momentum and ended up going along.

When we arrived at the mines, we found tons of entrances into the tunnels. I had no idea how many decades or centuries it had taken to dig them. Some were ancient, but others were new.

The golems had appeared in the newest tunnel, though the miners had been digging that one for years now. There were two entrances to the new tunnel and they met partway in. You could get to the deepest room where the golem had appeared by taking either.

The bozo rangers always used the same entrance, so Jaden's party used the other one to avoid trouble. It kept the other party from complaining that Jaden and the others had stolen their mark or something. Seemed like the right way to deal with those doofuses to me. Better to avoid them than beat them up.

A gamer learns to recognize a true bozo after a while. Bozos are self-centered, don't listen to others, are narcissistic, twist words to their own benefit, act rashly, and blame others for their own mistakes. I'd come across tons of them while playing my game, and it was better just to avoid them.

The entrances were a slight way off from the town, and it was pitch-black inside. Just when I was thinking we'd need light magic, Jaden put his hand on the wall near the entrance and the inside of the tunnel lit up.

Light mana gems, just like the Bear Tunnel. Mana lines connected light mana gems so that the tunnels could be lit up at what was basically the press of a switch. Then again, any average house in this world was outfitted with this stuff.

This tunnel was wide enough for a carriage to pass through with some room to spare. It seemed to continue pretty far in, but I couldn't tell how far from the entrance.

I used my bear map skill. It showed part of the tunnel's entrance: the map would be useful, but it only ever showed places I'd already been. I often thought of it as a kind of automapping tool.

Next, I used my bear detection skill. There were some golem signals up ahead. Since the map was incomplete, all I knew was that they were ahead on the dark part of the map—"the fog of war" we'd call it in the game. Right now, I couldn't tell if the signals meant they were in the same tunnel, one of the neighboring tunnels, or even down below us.

Jaden led the group into the tunnel. Mel and I followed, and Senia and Toya trailed us.

"It starts out with mud golems—then the rock golems start appearing further in."

"Mud and rock golems are a piece of cake to deal with, but the downside is that their mana gems aren't worth all that much."

Mud golems? Maybe this would be a good time to break out my bears to fight them. And speak of the devil...

A mud golem appeared the moment I thought that, right where I'd seen one of the golem signals show up earlier. It was about two and a half meters tall with thick arms and legs. Yeah, one whack from these guys would ruin your day at *least,* especially if you were just some miner trying to just do your job.

Jaden gave out orders to his party members and broke into a run.

It looked like they had a routine going. Mel lopped off the golem's arms using wind magic, although that wasn't enough to stop the mud golem in its tracks. Next up was Jaden, cutting off the golem's feet with his sword. Once its legs were cut off, the golem slouched forward and collapsed. Senia leaped onto its back while it was immobilized and stabbed it with a knife, then tore out its mana gem from the hole she'd made.

The mud golem crumbled on the spot. The whole thing had been a fluid operation.

Toya hadn't been standing idle either. While the others were fighting, he'd been acting as the lookout.

Without its gem, the golem had crumbled back into plain dirt. Apparently, the mana gem had been powering it, meaning we could do massive damage by hitting that weak point. Made sense to me.

KUMA
KUMA
KUMA
BEAR

151
The Bear Enters the Mines
Part Two

JADEN'S PARTY kept slaying the mud golems.

It looked to me like you could just slay mud golems with wind magic. Cutting off their arms and legs would immobilize them—though I guess that would immobilize anything, monster or no. But what would happen if we cut their heads off? Would that stop them? Or would they keep moving?

If Jaden and company only focused on cutting off each golem's limbs, maybe there was no point in cutting off the heads. We kept going further into the tunnel while I watched their fights.

Jaden and Toya fought with swords, Mel used magic, and Senia relied on daggers. They slayed mad mud golem, no problem. No wonder why they were C-Rank adventurers. I never had a chance to join the combat.

I looked at the bear map. It only displayed the part of the tunnel we'd already traveled.

Each tunnel fork was marked with a signpost so you could tell where to head for the exit.

This was what I'd picked up about the tunnels: Each entrance was assigned the letters A and B. Whenever there was a fork, each path was marked with a number, like 1, 2, or 3. According to Jaden, that was how they'd figure out where they were working. If someone said they were working "B-1-2-1," for instance, it was easy to figure out their location.

Still, I was bored. I really wanted to see just how strong golems could really get. Couldn't I slay just one? But nope, I never really got a turn since Jaden's party kept knocking them out. And what was I supposed to say, anyway? "Please, sir, may I pretty please kill a golem?" Super awkward.

They all kept on the lookout as we pressed on. I detected four golems up ahead.

We continued forward a bit and came into a wider space. There were three golems there...wait, three? Where was the fourth? I checked my detection; it seemed to be behind a large rock to our right. I guess it was in a blind spot. Jaden and the others had no idea.

They started running at the three golems in front of them. It didn't matter whether they were facing one golem, two, or three—the golems were no match for their coordinated assault.

They could easily defeat mud golems, no matter how many there were.

It looked like they hadn't noticed the last one. It wouldn't be so bad if I took that one, right? We were almost upon it and they hadn't even noticed it yet. I should totally take that one.

It *would* be weird for me to attack a golem I couldn't even see, though, so I decided to wait to make a move until it came into view.

After easily defeating the three golems, the party of three kept walking down the tunnel without minding the giant boulder. They didn't notice the hidden golem. I readied for attack...

But the moment the golem entered my field of vision, Jaden—who was walking in front of me—and Mel—who was beside me—reacted at the same time. They'd cottoned on fast. Maybe they'd heard it beforehand, or maybe they just had really quick reflexes? C-Rank adventurers, man.

Regardless, I'd already cast my wind magic. Right as the golem tried to come out from behind the boulder, my magic hit it and sliced off its head and all its limbs simultaneously. It was soft, as I expected. The sliced-and-diced chunks crumbled away, leaving only a mana gem behind.

Mud golems really weren't all that tough, then. Well, it *was* made of soil, so that was as sturdy as it could be. I hadn't even needed to imagine bears to strengthen my magic.

"Yuna, that was amazing," Mel called out. Both Jaden and Mel had noticed the golem too, and they'd been pretty quick on the uptake. I hadn't been able to tell whether Senia and Toya had gotten a chance to react to the golem though.

"But you did something weird just now. You got ready to attack before we could even see it," Senia commented. She'd been watching me from behind. Wow, she'd really been paying attention.

"The golem appeared right when you started moving, bear girl," Toya said.

Senia nodded. "You were quick to react."

So they *had* noticed. But I couldn't tell them about my bear detection skill though, so...

"You could say it was a woman's intuition?" I tried hedging.

"A woman's intuition?" Jaden looked dubious, but Mel grabbed onto my bear puppet paw.

"Of course. Women's intuition is *so* a thing, but Jaden and Toya insist it isn't."

"It definitely is a thing," Senia also agreed.

"Right, but it's just weird for someone to claim they sense a monster or here or over there or wherever without any evidence," Jaden said, which made Toya nod.

"And the only reason you can give is because of this women's intuition thing."

"Women's intuition has saved us in the past," Mel snapped, "and you know it."

The women chalked things up to women's intuition, and the guys didn't even believe it was real. I'd started a civil war with a single statement. Well, it wasn't like they were *actually* fighting, but it sure was a waste of time. I decided to change the subject.

"So, do golems keep moving around even after they lop off their heads?"

"Yeah. Golems will basically move no matter what part of them you slice off. There are two ways to stop them: One is to remove their mana gem. The other is to hit them with more damage than they can tolerate."

"More than they can tolerate?"

"So you know that the golems are powered by mana gem, right?" I'd mostly gotten that, so I nodded. "Well, the more damage you do to them, the less power their mana gem will have. Once all the power in that gem fizzles down to nothing, the golem goes kaput."

Hmm. So as long as you hit them with enough physical attacks, you could inflict damage on them until they couldn't move. If that was the case, you could slay rock and iron golems just by physically hitting them over and over again. Looked like I didn't even need to use my magic—I could go with a brute-force approach. I gripped my bear puppet into a fist.

I took the mana gem that had come from the defeated golem, and we pressed on down a gently sloping tunnel. I checked my bear map as we walked. Something changed on the map—the one I'd been using until now had vanished and was replaced with a new one. Interesting...when we moved from one level to another, the map changed too. It really was like the automap in the game.

Because the map had changed, I invoked my detection skill. More golems ahead.

"I think you'll be okay, but be careful, Yuna," said Jaden. "This is where the rock golems start coming out."

I nodded obediently. "Are they strong?"

"I guess they're about as tough as stone reinforced with a smidge of magic, but...I wouldn't call them quite like normal rocks. They move, after all."

I didn't really get what she meant with the reinforcement thing. What, that they were a little sturdier than the average rock? I doubted that a little bear magic couldn't handle it, but I hoped the group wouldn't mind me taking one to practice on.

Eventually, we finally encountered a rock golem—you know, the golems all cobbled together from rocks and stones? When I say "cobbled," though, I mean it: they kind of looked like they'd fall right apart if you punched one.

When the rock golem noticed us, it swung its arm, hurling a baseball-sized rock at us.

The blazing fast rock flew at a 160 kilometers per hour (or something like that, probably) at Jaden up on point. Mel stepped in front of Jaden and summoned a wall at a slight angle, deflecting the rock from us all. When the rock golem tried to throw a second, Jaden and Mel slipped out from behind the wall.

The rock golem locked onto Jaden and started to turn to face him. Then, as though she were fighting fire with fire, Mel produced a boulder the size of a soccer ball with her magic and smashed the golem's leg. The rock golem lost its balance, but it still swung its arm to desperately throw another stone. Senia stopped that quick: she threw her knife right into its joint. Jaden and Toya closed in instantly and attacked.

It wasn't long at all before the rock golem stopped moving and crumbled into a mountain of rocks and stones. The thing was a monster for sure, but it was nothing like any I'd seen so far.

Lots of rock golems showed up after that, but Jaden and the others made quick work of them. Mel broke their legs with magic, Senia threw her knives into their joints to slow the golems down, and finally, Jaden and Toya attacked from behind. None of them hesitated. Each of them understood what they had to do.

They were like an assembly line. It really reminded me of how high-level players operated, back in the game. You could turn the fight into a set pattern to make grinding for experience more efficient. I'd done that a ton myself. I'd even team with parties sometimes. Well, once in a while. I had *some* experience being in a party, even if it wasn't much.

I still wanted to take a stab at fighting a rock golem, though. Serendipitously, just as I thought that, we emerged into a slightly larger cavern that held five golems. Maybe I'd get a tiny piece of the action this time?

"Jaden, what do you want to do?" Mel asked. Up until now, they had only handled two golems at a time at most, but this was double trouble.

Jaden looked at me. "Could you take one, Yuna?"

"I guess I could."

Oh! Finally, my time to shine. *And* they were asking me to do it. I guess I'd gained their trust then. There were tons of things I wanted to try out, but first and foremost, I wanted to see how tough these things were. Maybe this called for some bear punches? I also wanted to see what magic could do to them, though...

"Thanks," said Jaden. "Once we take the others down, we'll be right there to help you out."

Everyone headed toward their respective rock golem. While I was hemming and hawing over how to go about attacking the thing, the rock golem started approaching me. I decided to dodge the golem's extended arm. I threw a firm bear punch into its chest...

And the rock golem went flying backward, struck the wall, and shattered. Curtains down, in three beautiful acts.

After a single bear punch.

I looked around to find the other four staring at me with blank expressions. (Which seemed pretty unpro-fessional, considering that they were engaged in combat themselves.) But it was only for a second, after which they immediately focused their attention back on the rock golems in front of them.

Okay, so I'd better help out, right? I headed toward the golems the four of them were fighting and fired off a few bear punches. The remaining four rock golems flew away, hit the walls, and crumbled.

Talk about weak. And the group was practically freaking out now...

"Yuna, you really are powerful."

"Just like the rumors say."

The two women came over.

"I guess you really must have killed a black viper and tigerwolves all on your own," Jaden admitted.

"I never would've thought a little bear girl could be so strong," said Toya.

Pssht. If this was all the rock golems amounted to, maybe an iron golem would be no trouble at all.

152
The Bear Enters the Mines
Part Three

EVER SINCE I'd one-hit the rock golem, Jaden and the others couldn't see me the same way.

"Where's all that power stored up in that little body of yours?" Toya said as he bopped me in the head a couple times from above. He was tall.

"I can barely believe you're a girl like me." Senia was touching my upper arms through my bear onesie. "Hmm, feels flabby."

Wait, *what* was flabby? The bear onesie? Or my arms?

Ehh, whatever. I shook the two of them off and plowed ahead. We'd changed the order of our lineup after the iron golem incident, so now weak little old me was heading the party with Jaden.

"We'll cover you, so relax," Mel had said earlier—and taken a step back.

It usually didn't bode well to make changes to a party halfway through a dungeon, but...I couldn't really argue against it, could I? We pushed on.

Still, those rock golems were way weaker than I'd expected. The only problem was that I couldn't hit them any harder than I had back then. I'd been pulling my punches, and I still wound up shaking pebbles and dirt free of the ceiling when the golems hit the walls.

"Well, the tunnel *is* reinforced with earth magic, so it probably won't collapse if you're hitting it a little."

They'd used magic on it like I had with the Bear Tunnel, but...I kinda thought the tunnel *had* collapsed just a little earlier from the force I'd used earlier. If I didn't hold back, this bear might wind up wrecking the joint.

In the end, I finished off rock golems with reserved bear punches that wouldn't damage the walls of the delicate tunnel.

"Looks like we've completely switched roles," Jaden said as he watched me take out a rock golem with a bear punch.

"Glad I didn't make fun of you that one time," Toya said.

Jaden laughed. "If you had, you sure would've ended up like those golems, Toya."

"It's okay," said Mel. "We would have made sure to put 'Here lies Toya, killed by a bear,' on your gravestone for you."

"Don't just kill me off!"

The three of them laughed. Toya did not.

We kept on through the tunnel without any issues before reaching the next level. Iron golems would appear from this point, they said. Since the golems became more powerful with each level change, it was *really* starting to feel like a dungeon. Sure, the game I'd played had those, but were there actually dungeons in this world too?

And how many? Could I explore more?

First step in my new level was, as before, using my detection skill. I detected iron golems.

Five golems waited in what seemed to be the deepest part of the tunnel. I wondered if those were the iron golems Jaden and the bozo rangers had mentioned? And beyond those things was that first golem, the one that might've started it all.

But...I wasn't picking up a golem further in. Was it on an even lower level?

Eventually, we came out into a cavern, and there it was towering at the center. It was the same size as the rock golems, but covered head to...toe?...in iron. Its arms were thick and strong as hammers—one hit would squash you like a fly.

If only you could talk to these things, you know? I'd recommend a career change. Maybe carpentry?

Anyway, this thing was built like a tank. It didn't seem like it would go down as easily as the rock golems—I couldn't just hit it. Maybe I could melt the iron if I used a fire bear, but using magic like that in a tunnel would be as good as suicidal. It'd turn the place into an oven, burn up all the oxygen, and it'd be game over for us.

I wondered if I could suffocate the things by wrapping their heads in water, but that probably wouldn't work. Or—oh, what if I splashed brine on them, causing them to rust up, so they couldn't move? But then we couldn't sell the iron...and how long does it take for things to rust, anyway?

Next up was wind magic, but the question was whether that could cut through iron. From what I'd heard, these things were sturdier than normal metals. Maybe I'd be able to lop through them with bear wing magic?

Earth magic...was a *maybe*. I could make bear golems to pin them down so we could attack them...but we had to have a *way* to attack them for that to work.

Finally, I could just avoid fighting entirely by burying them in a hole, but digging a random hole might weaken the structural integrity of the whole mine...and again, how would we get the iron? And let's say I did that anyway...well, somebody might dig them up someday and get hammered.

For now, I decided to watch how Jaden and the others fought the iron golems, so I'd have a good point of reference.

Jaden's party began preparing for battle.

First, Mel fired a clod of earth at the golem with magic—you could harden dirt by compressing it, and skilled mages could compress it more to make it even tougher. Wham! The golem's movements slowed for a moment. Toya tried attacking it then, but the golem deflected the attack with its arm. It was like clanging an iron column with a sword—no way to just cut through it.

When the iron golem was facing Toya, Senia circled around to its rear. She was holding a knife in each of her hands. Was she dual-wielding? But what was the point when Toya's sword hadn't worked?

Senia dashed to the iron golem in an instant and slashed at its leg. She wasn't able to lop it off entirely, but yeah—somehow, she had definitely cut into its thigh. Could you really do that? Kill an iron golem with knives?

"Senia has mithril knives," Mel explained to me when she saw my surprise. Okay, that made sense, especially given her rank.

Toya and Mel distracted the golem while Senia attacked from its blind spot. After she slashed the golem in the same spot about two or three times, the iron leg broke off, falling to the ground with a *clang*.

The one-legged golem lost its balance and fell over. Senia really had cut through that thick leg with a knife, and she looked way proud of it too.

Down by one leg, the golem was limping and thrashing when Jaden came down with his sword. The iron golem raised its arm to defend itself, but Jaden slashed down with his sword.

Wow...what could I even say? "Um. Is Jaden's sword also mithril?"

Mel nodded. "Yup. But it's not just like he can cut through an iron golem just because it's a mithril sword. Jaden can do that because of his skill with a sword. If Toya tried that, the blade would snap."

Made sense. If any nobody with a mithril sword could slice right through a golem, they'd give out the swords to D-Rank and E-Rank adventurers like candy. No, it was the combination of Jaden's ability with the mithril sword that made it all possible. It was their skill that made Jaden and his party C-Rank adventurers, not their gear. I mean, Senia had literally sliced through an iron golem with a knife. What could you even say to that?

"What about your sword, Toya?" I asked.

"It's a good sword, but it's not mithril."

Maybe that was why the golem had been able to fight it off—that and his skill, maybe. Then...where were *my* skills at? I'd used swords when I'd played the game. There'd been an assist function, so I'd picked up some things from playing. Thanks to my bear gear, I could wield both swords and magic at about the same level as I had in the game, but what did that mean, in practice, for my swordplay skills?

Sure, I could handle a sword the same way I had in the game, but was that really *skill*? If I had a mithril weapon, would I be able to take down an iron golem using the sword skills I had from the game?

I wanted to test it out, but I didn't have a mithril weapon.

Ugh, why couldn't I have one already?

The iron golem tried to stand up, even with a missing arm and leg, but that was a no-go. It swung its single arm and punched at Jaden, but he dodged and took several steps back, getting in an attack on the monster mid-dodge.

Toya groaned. "If I just had a mithril sword too, I could take down an iron golem."

"No way," Senia said bluntly. Toya opened his mouth to reply, but Senia beat him to it, "You borrowed Jaden's sword the other day and you could barely cut a piece of grass."

Toya just silently glubbed at her, his mouth opening and closing like a fish.

"Give you a mithril sword?" said Senia with a sneer. "Please, that'd be pearls before swine." Oof. Absolutely annihilated, Toya.

That whole time, Jaden was still dodging and slashing at the iron golem. The iron golem gradually slowed, then it finally collapsed. It'd been ruthlessly hacked up. Well, no one would be putting that thing up for display, that's for sure.

A wild thought had come to my mind watching Jaden's party battling. Just bear with me here for a second, but... what if *I* had a mithril weapon? I didn't know whether I could *wield* one, but it would be helpful when I couldn't rely on magic or my brute bear strength.

Senia put the mass of iron that the golem had become into an item bag. I looked at the destroyed golem, noting the mana gem in its chest. As long as you didn't care about selling the mana gem, couldn't you go straight for that instead of bothering with all the hack-and-slash?

Apparently not. "The location of the mana gem depends on the golem," said Jaden, "so you'd have a hard time destroying it."

"Really?"

"If we could do that, we would've already defeated those five iron golems a long time ago."

So no one-hit kills on these guys, then. Still, I wondered if there was a way to destroy it from the inside without damaging its exterior, sort of like with the black viper. Maybe I could make micro vibrations in the air, drive them into its body, and shatter it from within? Hmm. It was an idea, at least...

KUMA
KUMA
KUMA
BEAR

The Bear Enters the Mines
Part Four

AFTER RETRIEVING THE REST of the iron golem, Jaden told us to take a short break. There'd be more iron golems from this point on, so he wanted us to take a breather.

"So, Jaden, how far are we going today?" Toya asked after taking a deep swig of something.

"If we can, I want to get to the deepest point. Those five iron golems might not be there."

Unfortunately, they were definitely showing up on my detection skill. There was something else there that concerned me too, though...see, I'd detected five humans as well. Maybe the bozo rangers were here down with us.

Whoever they were, they weren't too far away from us. Maybe we'd bump into them if we kept moving forward. My bear map was still completely black, so I really didn't know where we'd cross paths. What I *did* know was that the bozo rangers were near the five golems. They'd run into the golems before we arrived.

While I was meditating over my bear map that only I could see, Jaden spoke to me. "Why so quiet?"

"I was thinking about how I'd like a mithril weapon." I couldn't tell him about my bear detection skill, but it wasn't *technically* a lie. "I actually went to the capital to get a mithril knife for butchering, but seeing yours and Senia's has got me wanting a mithril weapon too. Then, when I got to the capital, I got sent on a wild goose chase. By the end of it all, Sanya the guild master asked me to do this quest."

The quest had actually come from Ellelaura, but I don't think she'd want that getting around.

Mel frowned. "Let's get straight to the real issue: Will they actually send soldiers from the capital if we can't slay the golems? When's that supposed to happen?"

What was this, an interrogation?

"I didn't ask, but the castle put a rush on it. There might not be much time left on the clock." It probably depended on how I reported back to them, but I wasn't about to tell them that.

Jaden stood. "Looks like we'd better get to it quick then."

"You know what'd make all this go quicker?" said Toya as he stood up. "If I had a mithril sword. I'd take care of those iron golems, no problem."

"That joke's getting old already. No one's laughing at it anymore."

"Toya, no one's going to laugh when you make self-deprecating jokes like that."

"But I wasn't joking!" Toya yelled at Mel and Senia, who remained convinced he'd been pulling their legs.

"You need to polish your skills a little more for a mithril sword," Jaden said.

"Tsk." Toya shut up, seeming to accept it when it came from the party leader.

Man, though... I wonder how I'd do with a mithril sword? I'd come here to get mithril, and now it turned out I needed a mithril weapon to get mithril in the first place! Where was the game designer for this world? 'Cause I had some *notes*.

We went still deeper. When we ran into iron golems, Mel, the midfielder, shot off magic while Toya would distract them. While those two created an opening, Jaden and Senia would attack using their mithril weapons. Two more fell to that strategy.

We merged with another path. Could this be the

tunnel that the bozo rangers had been going down? I checked my detection skill, and...

Huh?

The five iron golems had disappeared. They had definitely been there the last time I checked, but now they were nowhere to be seen. Had the bozo rangers really taken them out? But *they'd* disappeared too. Were they on another level?

The party crept forward and peered into the cave where the five iron golems should have been. It's not like I could just tell them not to worry about it, so I just followed behind them instead.

"They're not here," said Jaden.

Toya nodded. "Aye."

"But there are signs of a fight," said Mel.

Sure enough, there *were* signs that there'd been a fight all over. A wall had collapsed and the ground had been gouged out. This cave wasn't going to come down on our heads, right? The last thing I wanted was to be buried alive.

"Do you think it was Barbould's party?" asked Mel.

Barbould...? Oh, right, Bozo Red. I was pretty determined to just call him that in my head, so it'd taken me a sec.

"I can't think it'd be anyone else," said Jaden.

"Did they really slay all five of them?" asked Toya.

"They're unpleasant people, but they're nothing to scoff at," said Senia.

So the bozo rangers could hold their own in a fight. Too bad I hadn't shown up earlier so I could've seen it.

"Jaden, what do you want to do?" Mel asked. She kept watch on our surroundings as we talked it over.

"Barbould cleared the path for us, so we'll keep heading forward. We'll be better off if we've got more information, no matter how little."

"And if Barbould spots us?" asked Toya.

"We don't let him," said Senia.

"I'd rather avoid trouble," said Jaden, "but we're adventurers, so we've gotta go."

"We can head back if they grumble at us," said Mel.

So, working with them to finish the quest wasn't even on the table, huh? Not that I could blame anybody. If we did team up with the bozo rangers, I was pretty sure I'd end up accidentally shooting magic at the backs of their heads.

We continued down the passage again and changed levels, and my bear map updated. Five signals, which seemed to be the bozo rangers, showed up with a monster signal...the signal of a mithril golem.

Sounds of battle echoed along the passage as we went on.

"Damn, this golem's *hard*."

"It's magic-resistant, too."

"Engai, do something."

"Do *what*, exactly?"

The bozo rangers were fighting in a cavern.

Bozo Red slashed with a sword, but it bounced off the golem. Bozo Blue stabbed with a spear, but it bounced off too. Bozo Green went with a giant hammer, but nope, *boing*. Bozo Black blasted earth magic, but it bounced right off. Bozo White fired wind magic at it, but—well, that bounced off too.

The bozo rangers' offense was ineffective. The mithril golem repelled both physical and magical attacks. Regardless, the bozo rangers kept attacking. It wasn't like they were weak, you know? They were quick on their feet compared to Deboranay, who was in Rank D, and their teamwork seemed all right.

But they weren't dealing any damage. The bozo rangers hammered away at the mithril golem, doing nothing at all but refusing to give up.

Jaden's group watched, shocked, as the bozo rangers fought the mithril golem. I think they hadn't noticed it *was* mithril.

"Is that an iron golem?"

"I think it is, but..."

"Barbould is wielding a mithril sword, right?"

"Maybe the golem's been reinforced with magic."

The golem repelled a hefty attack from Bozo Red.

"Damn! What's with this thing? It's indestructible."

Bozo Black hit it from the side with another large stone...which promptly shattered without leaving a scratch. The golem was unharmed—and that was no exaggeration. Mages were especially at a disadvantage here: they could only use certain types of magic, and they had to be especially careful about friendly fire.

Physically attacking it didn't work. Magic didn't, either. How was anybody supposed to slay a mithril golem, then?

The bozo rangers eventually noticed us watching their losing fight. "What'd you come here for?"

"We're just here to watch," said Jaden. "If you guys wound up dead, we thought we'd take over and handle it for you, but it looks like you've got it covered."

"Pssht! Nothing's going to do *me* in. Go on, scram! If you wanna be an audience to our fight, I'll charge you for tickets!" He waved his sword at us. "You even brought your pet bear with you?!"

He was talking about me, wasn't he? Maybe I'd summon Kumayuru to attack him from behind.

"Okay, just to be certain, you're sure you don't need a hand?"

"No!" Bozo Red snapped.

"Got it. Well, I guess we'll just head back. Don't worry, if you die, we'll make sure the guild knows all about your fight."

"Like we'd die!" Bozo Red roared, rushing at the golem.

Personally, I wish I could've watched them fight more, but Bozo Red was clearly going to make this a whole *thing,* so we left them to it.

A mithril golem, though...now that seemed like one problematic monster. I usually used brute-force attacks, so I'd end up in the same situation as Bozo Red. Mithril weapons were right out, because I sadly didn't own one. That left magic, but I'd be way limited in the tunnels.

"No way they'll be able to beat that thing," Jaden said as we walked.

"Yup, not a chance."

"What was it?" Toya asked the group.

"I'm sure it was tougher than the iron golems we fought so far."

"I don't even want to imagine something more resilient than an iron golem."

"Barbould couldn't even scratch it with his mithril sword."

"So he's not a great swordsman then?"

"He's got a rotten personality, but he knows how to handle a mithril blade."

"And even *he* couldn't kill it with a sword."

"Then wouldn't it have been better to help them?" I asked. If it was so impossible with just one party, why not join forces?

"He turned us down, so we can't help him."

"That's just how it is. We would help if they asked for it, but if they don't, we won't. That's the unspoken agreement between adventurers."

"When you help another party, figuring out how to divvy up loot and rewards gets tricky. Of course, we'd ignore all that and move to help them at once if they were in *actual* danger."

"And get told off by Barbould after."

Adventurers were workers, not superheroes, and the golems were just another job. We weren't going to get a paycheck by rescuing the bozos, you know?

So they didn't even consider the possibility of fighting alongside the bozo rangers, and it cut both ways: The bozo rangers would never ask for help. They'd entirely ruled out the possibility of working together, even if we could've finished the job together. The same kind of thing had happened in the game too. The fewer the people, the bigger the cut.

If everyone said there was no point in working with the bozos, I guess it wasn't really worth thinking about.

Honestly, even *I* felt tempted to monopolize the mithril golem.

We left the bozo rangers and their fight and made for home. Since I wanted to complete my map, I asked if we could go home with the path the bozo rangers had taken. Jaden's party was cool with it.

After returning from the mines, we stopped by the end to get a bite to eat. "Well," I started, "what do you want to do, Jaden?"

"About what?"

"About that golem. Didn't look like Barbould's party could kill it."

"Yeah, that thing's invincible."

Toya nodded. "Even *I* wouldn't be able to slay it with a mithril sword," he said.

(Everyone ignored Toya.)

"If Barbould's party defeats it for us," said Jaden, "the quest would be completed. If they can't, we just contact the guild."

"I guess that's all there is to it."

He nodded. "It really doesn't sit right with me, but that's the way it's done. Not much we can do."

Fair enough. How would *we* defeat the mithril golem, then?

If it just weren't down in those tunnels, I could have smashed the thing to pieces. As it was, though, I wasn't super into causing a massive cave-in. My OP bear abilities were useless in cramped quarters.

They wouldn't count it as a kill if I just buried the thing, would they? No, burying it wouldn't suffocate it, and that wouldn't stop whatever was causing the golems to appear.

Well, whatever. I needed that mithril ore. That was why I'd come out here.

We were resting and drinking tea after the meal when there was a commotion at the entrance.

"Damn it, how're we even supposed to beat that thing?"

"What kind of golem is magic-resistant anyway?!"

"That thing's impenetrable."

"I'm out of mana."

"I'm starving. Let's get some grub."

The bozo rangers had made their entrance. Looked like they'd made it back alive.

"You actually made it back," said Jaden, practically reading my mind.

"Like we'd let that thing kill us!"

"So did you slay it?" Jaden asked them deliberately, even though it was obvious from their earlier conversation and the look on their faces.

"You losers showed up and threw us off! We'll let that slide this time."

Oh, interesting. *They* were going to let it slide, huh?

"Sorry about that. I never thought you'd get thrown off by something so small. You're all *so* powerful, aren't you?"

"Tsk." Barbould had no comeback, or at least nothing that wouldn't just make things worse for him.

"Enough playing around. What actually happened in there?"

Barbould's party sat down in some empty chairs nearby. "That thing's impossible. Physical attacks, magical attacks, none of them leave a scratch...or if they've done anything at all, it's not enough to matter. If we kept pushing, we'd run out of stamina and mana way before it did."

"You're saying we can't slay it?"

"I'm saying you'd best be ready for that."

"And you? You're just giving up?"

"Not worth my time. Iron golems are more cost-effective anyway. I mean, you losers saw the fight, didn't you?"

"I guess we'll pass on it too. Not like we have a way of beating it either; we were actually hoping you'd take it down for us."

"Heh, sorry to disappoint."

"I guess we have to report this to the guild," said Jaden, going on to explain what I'd told him earlier.

"You think the capital's soldiers, mages, and knights'll be able to take it down?"

"They've got the manpower and the tools to do it."

"Well, we'll use the iron golems to grind for some cash until the soldiers from the capital get here."

"Thanks for the info, Barbould. Barkeep! A round of drinks for Barbould's party—on us."

"C'mon, only *one* round?"

"I'd treat you to another if you told us how to beat that thing."

"If we knew that, we wouldn't bother talking to you. The thing would be slayed already."

Barbould and Jaden were cracking themselves up now. Hold on, weren't they enemies, or...? Had I missed something? Was this just an adventurer thing?

Jaden's party and the bozo rangers spent the night trying to drink one another under the table. Me, I spent *my* night under some comfy covers in bed, thank you very much.

KUMA
KUMA
KUMA
BEAR

154
The Captured Princess
Part One

YUNA LEFT ME, her round bear tail wiggling into the distance.

Why had things turned out this way?

Maybe it had all started when Yuna asked me to butcher the black tiger. It was tough, and I couldn't skin it with my knife.

See, when living monsters die, the tough mana covering their bodies disappears. The supply from their mana gems goes away, their hide goes soft, and I can get to work. But the black tiger's pelt was too tough for me to butcher even with my knife! I guess it didn't help that I'm not very strong, but for the most part, greater monsters just need to be butchered with better tools.

I told Yuna so too, and Yuna suddenly said we were going to go buy a knife that could butcher the black tiger.

I was pretty sure a steel knife would have worked, but Yuna got set on a mithril knife. Those things are *way* expensive. Obviously, I said no, thank you, but she wouldn't listen! Yuna said we might need one next time. What was that supposed to even mean? What was Yuna going to have me butcher next?

It was terrifying just thinking about it!

Mr. Gold's blacksmith shop in Crimonia didn't have mithril knives to sell, but Yuna didn't stop there. She said that she would take me with her to the capital. Most people can't do that, but Yuna has this crazy bear door in her house. When you go through, you appear in the capital suddenly—it's so weird! I couldn't believe Yuna had something so amazing!

We went to the Merchant Guild and asked where the blacksmith was. On the way, um, we ran into Noa's sister—you know, Shia? Shia took us to the blacksmith, because she'd gone before.

We made it to the blacksmith without any problems, but we still couldn't get a mithril knife. There were monsters in the mines, so they couldn't get any ore.

But Yuna didn't give up. Next up, we had to go to the Adventurer Guild. When the adventurers saw Yuna, they were up in arms. I admit, I was so scared that I hid behind Yuna...

I thought we would get in a fight, but Sanya the guild master came over and told the adventurers off for us. You bet they got real quiet then. Sanya was so *cool!*

Sanya told us what had happened in the mines. It looked like we couldn't get a mithril knife. Kinda sad, but it wasn't like I really needed one yet.

Right when we were about to give up and go home, Lady Ellelaura came in. She asked Yuna to slay the golems that had appeared in the mines. Yuna said no at first, but she really did want that mithril knife...so she took the job.

Since Yuna was going away for work, I guess I had to just go home and wait in Crimonia? Since I could use the bear door, I could go home right away. But then Lady Ellelaura said the *unthinkable.*

"Well then, I'll take Fina to my house while you're out."

Lady Ellelaura grabbed me. I looked at Yuna, begging her to save me. She looked just as fidgety as I felt.

We couldn't say anything about the mystery bear door that went to Crimonia. Yuna didn't look like she knew what to do either. If she went on the job by herself, then I'd be alone. That was the last thing I wanted.

But then Yuna told Lady Ellelaura, "Please take care of her."

Yuna! I shouted at her inside my head.

Because the bear door was our secret, I couldn't just say I could go home to Crimonia, not by myself. And I couldn't go with Yuna if she was going to be slaying monsters either. There wasn't a choice at all, really. I ended up staying behind in the capital.

Even thinking about staying at a noble's house as a commoner made me sick to my stomach. I asked if I could stay by myself in Yuna's bear house, but Yuna and Lady Ellelaura both said no.

But—but I'm fine being alone! No fair...

Yuna stayed over for just a night before leaving me behind to slay golems. I was worried about her, but I also had to worry about myself. If I messed up, I'd never live it down.

I decided to keep out of the way and stay in my room like a good girl...but I still didn't get any peace. Lady Ellelaura and the maid, Surilina, came in, even though I was trying to be good! I had a bad feeling about this.

Surilina was carrying a ton of pretty dresses on hangers. Were these from when Lady Shia was small? Or were they Lady Noa's clothes? And who was going to wear them?

"I wonder which one will look best," said Lady Ellelaura.

"M'lady, what do you think of this one?"

"Very nice, but don't you think this is better?"

"Yes, I think that will look lovely!"

On Lady Noa or on Lady Shia? Or...or...oh, who was I kidding? They kept looking at me. Just thinking about it gave me a nervous stomach ache.

What I knew right now was that I was in danger.

Lady Ellelaura picked up an outfit and looked at me. "Fina, how about we get you changed?"

She started to approach me. Her smile scared me. Yuna wasn't here to save me. I had to say no to her myself. Just thinking about what would happen if I got those clothes dirty or did anything to them made me shudder.

"I already have clothes on, so I'm okay," I tried really hard to tell her, N*o, thank you*.

"Tssk, tssk. No, my dear, those clothes simply will *not* do. and haven't you been wearing those since yesterday?"

"They're not *that* dirty," I said, taking a quick step back...but Lady Ellelaura and Surilina took two steps toward me.

"That's no good. A girl like you needs to dress nicely."

Yuna, save me...

Lady Ellelaura and Surilina started coming over to me

again. I wished I could ask Lady Shia to save me, but she was at the academy. There wasn' no one here to come to my aid.

I took another step back and bumped into the bed that was behind me. I was stuck. The two of them still kept walking toward me.

I had nowhere else to run.

"I can't wear such nice clothes. I wouldn't look right in them."

"Oh pish, that's not true. I'm sure you'll look adorable."

"Yes, I do agree. You're *already* so adorable."

It was no use. They had me surrounded on both sides. I couldn't escape.

"But what if I got them dirty? They look like such expensive clothes." Maybe that would work

"It's fine. I won't get angry," said Lady Ellelaura.

"Oh, and don't worry about getting them dirty. I'll wash them, so it'll be fine."

"But..." But what? What could I say to escape?

Yuna, save me...

But she was far away, out of reach of my pleas.

"..."

In the end, I lost the clothes war.

The outfit did have cute frills, and it felt nice, too. The

fabric was really fine. Surilina promised to take care of it if I got anything dirty, but what if I accidentally tore it?

One word was on my mind: compensation. I absolutely could not tear these clothes or get any dirt on them. My stomach ached with how scared I was, but I soldiered on. I'd stay as motionless as a doll in my room until Yuna came back. Yup, that seemed like a good plan.

"Well, Fina, let's head out."

"Wha—" What a move! It was over in seconds...but I couldn't give up yet. "I'll stay home and watch the house. I can wait for Yuna to come back."

"You're a guest; we could never ask that of you. If Miss Yuna returns, I shall notify you."

"And Yuna already left," said Ellelaura. "As talented as she is, she won't be back *that* quickly."

That was true, I guess. In the end, I couldn't figure out how to say no, and I had to go out with Lady Ellelaura.

But where were we going?

Wait, was that the *castle?*

Mom... if I get sentenced to death, I'm sorry.

Or maybe not...? No, I could make it. If I saw nobles in the castle, I had to do my very absolute best not to do anything rude...

That is, if I wanted to make it home *alive!*

155
The Captured Princess
Part Two

I ARRIVED WITH LADY ELLELAURA at the castle. This was my second time here, but I was still nervous. Yuna had been with me last time, and she wasn't here now.

"Is there anywhere you'd like to go, Fina?"

"Um..."

What was I supposed to say? I didn't even know what there was inside the castle. I only knew the places they showed me last time. All I knew was that I didn't want to see knights in their training ground. Too scary.

"I'm not sure..." I was so nervous, I could hardly think. *Please get back soon, Yuna!*

"Now don't be so nervous. If anyone tried to hurt you, I'll fight them in Yuna's place—why, I'd even fight the king himself. So don't fret."

Don't fret? How could I not fret? What if the king and Lady Ellelaura really *did* fight because of me? My stomach ache got worse.

"It'll be fine. Come, now," said Ellelaura and grabbed my hand.

Wh-where were we going? Not to where the king is, right?

But the place Ellelaura took me to was a beautiful blooming garden.

"It's so pretty..."

It looked like the blooming garden of a castle, straight from a picture book, but...this really *was* a castle. If I hadn't met Yuna, I would probably never have made it to the capital, let alone gotten into the castle. A commoner like me could never dream of seeing such sights.

There were lots of flowers I had never seen before blooming in the flowerbeds. They were different from the flowers that bloomed in the forest. It made me feel like a princess. Maybe God had prepared this for me, so I could see it before I died. Thank you very much, God...

But wait, no, I could make it back. There was still hope. Mom, Shuri, and Dad were waiting for me. I couldn't die in a place like this! I looked at the flowers. They were... really nice and calming.

Red, blue, pink, yellow—there were so many pretty flowers in bloom.

Little by little, I felt a bit better. Maybe I really *could* wait here without seeing anyone. If I did, I really might not run into any nobles if I were careful.

(That wasn't true, but it was a nice idea.)

"Taking a break, are we, Ellelaura?"

While I was looking at the flowers, someone came and started talking to Ellelaura. Another noble? Well, I looked over where the voice came from, and...it was someone much, much more powerful that. He was the man who had come to Yuna's house the other day.

He was the king! Wh-what was I going to do? Nobles were bad enough, but...yeah, I guess I really was going to die here.

Or even worse: If I offended the king, I might not be the only one who would die. He might even kill the rest of my family. And if I ran, what would he do then?

Oh, Yuna, save me...

"Today is my day off."

"Then what are you doing at the castle?"

"I'm taking a stroll with her today."

Lady Ellelaura put her arms around me. I was frozen, unable to make so much as a peep.

"Hrm? I think I've seen her somewhere before."

"Maybe you've seen her with Yuna?"

"Ah, yes, she was the girl at Yuna's house."

The king looked at me, and I felt like I was going to melt into a bubbly puddle of nerves.

"M-my name is Fina." Offering my name wouldn't get me killed, right?

"Much more polite than Yuna, I see." The king reached out his hand and patted my head. The king himself, right next to me, patted my head. I was sure I'd used up the last of my luck.

This was it. Goodbye, Mom. Take care, Shuri. Dad, please take care of everybody.

Ellelaura chuckled. "Oh, don't be rude to poor Yuna."

"You know, that girl has some nerve. She comes to the castle but never greets *me*. Who does that?"

"Well, that's because she comes here for Lady Flora."

"Precisely! When I see the girl in Flora's room, she has this look in her eyes like I'm an intruder. That girl looks at me and doesn't see a king at all."

Oh, no. Was she really doing that to the king?! Yuna! She was going to get herself killed. I had to warn Yuna when I saw her—*if* I saw her. Had to make it out of the castle alive to tell her...

"Well, she seems to be like that with everyone. When

I saw Cliff the other day, he said the same thing. Don't pretend; you find her as charming as the rest of us."

"Well, she *does* treat my little girl well. And she's saved us more than once. Most important of all, she brings such scrumptious delights."

Whoa, Yuna fed the king? I know she served us food back at home, but...wow.

Then again, everything Yuna made was delicious.

It looked like the king had forgotten about me, since he was so focused on talking about Yuna. Maybe I really would make it out of here without offending him. But just as I thought that...

"It was Fina, right?" the king suddenly said to me.

"Ye-aaaaaah."

Oh, no. I didn't mean it to come out like that! I was just so surprised, I—I didn't think the *king* would want to talk to me. I wasn't ready. How could I be so careless when my life depended on how this went? So stupid, Fina!

"Now, don't startle the poor child. Your face is already scary enough, Your Majesty."

"Such a casual insult! Well, I didn't mean to frighten her. I just wanted to know what she is to Yuna."

Oh? I...I didn't know, really. Were we friends? Or did

I work for her? I answered with the one thing I knew, the one thing that was sure:

"Yuna saved my life."

Yeah. If Yuna hadn't been there, I would have died.

"She saved your life?" the king asked.

He seemed curious, so I started telling the story of how I met Yuna. I don't know how, but I managed to get it all out without messing up.

"Ah, an encounter in the woods? Now that's surprising in an entirely different way."

I remembered being relieved that I was saved and really confused about lots of things when Yuna had shown up dressed as a bear.

The king paused for a moment and looked around. "Is Yuna not here?"

"Not today," said Ellelaura. "She headed to the mines for a job with the Adventurer Guild. I'm looking after Fina at my house in the meantime."

"The mines? Oh, I heard a report about that. Golems in the mines, yes? I've got a petition to send the soldiers if the Guild can't handle it."

"Then read it fully, Your Majesty. We *would* be mobilizing the army, after all."

"The operative word being *would*. We've got Yuna headed there, haven't we? We need no army."

Wow. The king really trusted Yuna.

Ellelaura nodded. "Yes. This *is* Yuna, after all."

"Right. Who could suspect such an appearance could hide such power?"

"She's simply adorable, isn't she?"

Uh-huh. I thought she was cute too.

"Now, Ellelaura, what's next on the docket for you?"

Were we leaving? Please? Even being near the king was too much to handle. I was practically going to faint... and it was almost lunch too! Maybe we could head back to the mansion now? I felt way more at home at Lady Ellelaura's mansion than I did in the castle. I gave Lady Ellelaura a pleading look.

"Are you hungry, Fina?"

She understood? I nodded a little.

"In that case, I have a souvenir from Yuna I need to hand off. Let's go to Lady Flora's room, shall we?"

"Is it edible?" the king asked.

"It's for lunch."

"Then I'll accompany you."

Wait, he was going to...maybe I'd misheard them? We weren't going to just...go to the princess's room and have lunch with the king, were we?

Nope. We were. Lady Ellelaura brought me to Flora's room.

Oh, Yuna, when will you rescue me?!

Several hours passed, but we did get back to the mansion in one piece. We even ate lunch together with Lady Flora and the king, though I didn't remember how anything tasted. And when the queen came in...my mind totally shut down.

I was back home and still alive. That meant I hadn't done anything wrong. I'd won!

I collapsed on the bed...

And Yuna would come to rescue me soon too, right? Right?

Kwoom, kwoom, kwoom, kwoom, kwoom.

Oh? That mysterious sound...where was it coming from?

It sounded familiar. I pulled out a bear doll from the item bag Yuna had given me. It really was the bear that was crooning! This was called a "bear fone," and it was a magical device that could be used to talk to someone far away. I poured mana into the bear fone I was holding.

"Hey, Fina. Can you hear me?"

"Yuna?!"

"You okay over there?"

"Yuna, it was so terrible. Lady Ellelaura made me

change into beautiful clothes, then she took me to the castle and we met the king. And then we had lunch with them, the king and queen!"

"So...the usual, then?"

"Maybe for you, Yuna, but I was so nervous that I couldn't even taste the bread I was eating."

"Did you have fun, at least?"

"Um, no? No! No. Yuna, tell me how *your* job is going. That's what's important."

"Ehh. I only just arrived today, so I don't have much to say."

"Really?"

"Yep. I'll try getting back quick, so you all have fun sightseeing in the capital until then. Hey, why don't you buy some souvenirs for Tiermina and the others?"

Yuna had loaned me all that money and even told me to use it how I wanted...and it was a *lot* of money. When I tried to give it back, she forced me to take it anyway. Lady Ellelaura fed me at the mansion, so what was I going to use it on? I was too scared to walk around the capital alone, too. I definitely wasn't going to go shopping.

"Please come back soon, Yuna."

"Roger that! I'll come back as soon as I can."

Yuna's voice faded away. Hearing her voice had made me feel better, even if I still really didn't understand how we were talking together though. I put away my bear fone, just as Surilina came to call me down for dinner.

156
The Bear Enters the Mines
Part Five: The Golem Chronicles

IMMEDIATELY ESCAPED to my room after Jaden's group and the bozo rangers started drinking in the dining room. Drunk people are the worst. You can't reason with them, and they always wanted to get in these annoying fights. You see a lot of that when staying in inns.

The best way to deal with drunks was to never involve yourself with them in the first place, no matter what world you're in.

I locked the door tight to keep any drunks from wandering into my room. Once I was sure no one would barge in, I sat down on my bed and wondered what I'd do now.

Jaden and the bozo rangers had basically given up on beating the mithril golem, right? Sure, soldiers would head our way if Jaden's party told the Adventurer Guild that they couldn't handle the golems, but it would take a while for them to get here.

If I was going to slay the mithril golem, I'd need to move faster than them.

No way was I going to hand that mithril golem over to the kingdom. If I could just figure out a way to beat that thing, I could have all the mithril for myself. I had to slay it before the soldiers.

But after seeing the bozo rangers fight the thing, I knew it wouldn't be easy. Plus, there were those five iron golems right before the mithril golem. Since I didn't have a mithril weapon in the first place, it would be a nightmare to fight them in the tunnel—what if there was a cave-in?

I stood up.

There was one thing I hadn't tried yet. One trick that might just work. But I was going to have to test my theory tonight.

I set up a bear transportation gate in my room.

Where did it lead? We'll get to that.

Fwunk fwunk.
Something hit my cheeks. Too sleepy. Ugh.
Fwunk fwunk.

I'd stayed up pretty late while testing my golem-slaying strategy. Didn't I deserve just a little more sleep?

Fwunk fwunk.

Even though I'd gotten back late, Jaden and the others were still partying it up in the dining room.

Fwunk fwunk.

Can you imagine? Weren't they tired after fighting all day? I guess that's why they were adventurers. Inexhaustible energy.

Fwunk fwunk.

I guess people who make C-Rank have that kind of stamina.

Fwunk fwunk.

"Fine, I'm up already, jeez!" I grabbed Kumayuru and Kumakyu's paws. Kumayuru and Kumakyu had been slapping me from either side for a while now. Sure, I wasn't technically feeling *exhausted* thanks to my white bear outfit, I was still sleepy. That was kind of a plus about the white bear outfit, if you ask me: It still let me sleep. And I *love* sleep! Can you imagine not being able to sleep?

But it wasn't like I could spend the whole day on it, so I got up.

"Morning, Kumayuru. Morning, Kumakyu." I patted their heads and stretched out. Sleepy or not, I had to get to work. There I was, fifteen years old with a job. Guess this world was rubbing off on me, huh? I got out of bed and swapped my white outfit for black.

I headed to the dining room, which reeked of alcohol. The whole place smelled like the inside of a bottle.

"Oh, you're up early, Miss Bear." The proprietress came out from the kitchen.

"Good morning. It smells a lot like alcohol in here," I greeted her, covering my nose with my bear puppet.

"Those idiots were drinking into the early morning. My husband was supposed to handle it—I went to bed, but he didn't get in until morning. The fool partied with them all through the night, and now he's sleeping it off. I'll forgive him this time, but next time, he's in for it."

Still, she smiled as she opened the windows. A pleasant breeze swept in.

"We'll air it out, so please bear with it for now. In exchange, I'll give you extra breakfast on the house."

I plopped down in a chair, yawning. No one was in the cafeteria, possibly because it was still early. Besides Jaden's party and the bozo rangers, there were merchants staying here to buy ore from the town. Still, I was the only one in the cafeteria.

Since there was no one to talk to, I lounged around while waiting for breakfast. The air cleared over time and it stopped smelling like booze eventually. The proprietress brought my meal over after a while.

"Here we are. Sorry to keep you waiting."

"Thank you very much."

"What are you going to do today? You're one of the adventurers, but...I don't think Jaden and the others will be getting up for a while."

"Hmm. I think I'm gonna head over to the mines on my own."

"On your *own*?!"

"Yup. I want to wrap things up fast so I can go home."

"*Wrap things up?* But even Jaden, Barbould, and the others couldn't do it. A young girl like you can't go out there on her own? No, it's too dangerous."

Yeah, anybody *would* assume that about some girl in a bear suit. Since she genuinely seemed worried for me, I took her concerns seriously. "But you'd have problems if the mines stayed like this forever, right?"

"Well, sure. If the miners wind up out of a job, they won't come in for a drink anymore. And if they don't come in for a drink..." She told me that they'd already lost a few customers who came in after work. I guess everybody likes a cold one, no matter your world.

"But that's no reason for a young lady like you to go out and fight monsters."

"I'm not going to put myself in harm's way. Tell you what, I'll run away if I can't deal with anything."

"You promise? Then come straight back here if it gets too dangerous, you here? Still, a girl like you trying to be an adventurer..." She shook her head.

I thanked the concerned proprietress and, after chowing down on my huge breakfast, headed to the mines on my own. It was early in the morning, so there weren't many people walking around outside and I didn't have any annoying encounters on the way to the mines.

Time to see if sacrificing all that sleep last night had been worth it.

I headed into the tunnel alone. Jaden and the others weren't here this time to guide me, but I'd been sure to fill out my bear map all the way to the mithril golem.

Mud golems emerged as I progressed down the tunnel, but I chopped them with wind magic and continued on my way.

The tunnels were quiet and it was kinda lonely. Toya wasn't here to say silly things, and Senia wasn't here with her sharp tongue. Jaden wasn't here giving out instructions either. Mel wasn't here to talk straight with me. Even comparing it to the wilderness I'd come out of... there was no wind here, no sound of birds chirping. I hadn't expected the quiet.

I wasn't going to demand music or anything, but I wanted something comforting, so I stretched out my arms and summoned Kumayuru and Kumakyu. My bears nuzzled me.

There we go. Loneliness, begone!

Kumayuru and Kumakyu tagged along with me to my left and right, which cheered me right up. I had to admit I was super grateful to the god of this world for giving me these two as my summons.

I kept plowing forward with my bears, chopping up all the mud golems with wind magic as I went. They really did respawn, huh? But when? Maybe they came back a few hours after being defeated, or maybe they revived at a specified time? No matter the reason, no way could the miners work around a daily monster respawn.

Once I was done with the mud golem level, I went down to deal with the rock golems. I obliterated the first few with bear punches, but Kumayuru and Kumakyu looked like they wanted a turn.

"Fine by me. I'll leave the next ones to you."

They took on a golem each, easily defeating them with literal bear punches.

That's right, folks: they're cute, strong, soft, warm, and even convenient for travel. Every household could use one, and I was lucky enough to have two.

Since my bears had handled the rock golems so easily, I hadn't had a chance to do anything. But once we went down this slope, we'd be on the level where the iron golems appeared, and I'd have a chance to use the magic I'd sacrificed sleep to master.

We continued down the tunnel. I spotted an iron golem before long and signaled to Kumayuru and Kumakyu to stay put as I headed toward it on my own.

Let's hope this works...

As I formed an image in my head, yellow and blue light coiled around my black bear puppet along with a crackling sound.

Electricity magic.

Electricity was effective against a metal like iron. If I could flood the iron golem with electricity, the current might travel through its body and obliterate the mana gem inside.

Did electricity magic even exist in this world, you might ask? Well, it sure wasn't in the beginner's magic book I'd bought earlier. My guess was they didn't even have a *concept* of electricity. If they knew it at all, it was in the form of lightning...but as for what they thought lightning was, or what caused it, they seemed to have no idea.

Hence, no lightning magic. That was my guess, at least.

It had been with that theory in mind that I'd snuck out of the inn to practice my electricity magic. I wasn't quite sure how to visualize it at first—in games and anime, they'd recite a spell or something and lightning would burst from a cloud, but the magic in this world was tied to manipulating your own mana. You couldn't just pull lightning from the sky.

Instead, I'd pictured gathering an electric charge into my bear puppet. Visualizing my mana as electricity turned out to be simple; a current immediately coiled around my bear puppet and began to crackle.

My experiment was a success, though I couldn't aim with much accuracy when I fired the electricity from my glove at range. It was pretty late by that point, though, so I settled for perfecting my static bear punches instead.

Once I'd completed my crash course in electricity, my static-charged bear puppet was crackling away.

So far, I'd only practiced on rocks—no monsters. I wanted to see how powerful this golem was, so I threw a weak static bear punch at it. A *real* weak one. I mean, I barely tapped it.

With a soft *whump* and a loud fizzle, the thing just... collapsed. I barely pushed it and the golem fell backward onto the ground, motionless.

I kicked its leg. No reaction. Awesome.

It seemed like the electricity really *had* flowed through the golem and destroyed its mana gem. I packed the iron golem away into my bear storage and plowed forward, searching for the next one.

157
The Bear Enters the Mines
Part Six: Mithril Golems

I'D BECOME A REAL ONE-PUNCH BEAR after mastering my static bear punch. Just one hit on an iron golem knocked it out, crackling with electricity on the ground. Piece of cake.

I could tell Kumayuru and Kumakyu were bored walking beside me since I hadn't been giving them a turn, but I was just happy to have their company.

"Help me out if I'm having trouble, okay?" I asked them. Anything could happen in a fight, after all. That must've made them feel better, since they gave me a *kwoom* in reply and seemed to gain a skip in their step.

I didn't *really* need to ask. Kumayuru and Kumakyu always came to my rescue if I was in a pinch.

I patted their heads as they walked to my left and right. It must've seemed out of the blue to them, because they gave me little confused head-tilts, but they seemed to enjoy the attention. We continued down the tunnel.

Kumayuru and Kumakyu didn't need to intervene since we didn't run into anything dangerous. Four iron golems went down, leaving only the five more on the way to the mithril golem. The bozo rangers had defeated them the day before, but they'd all respawned, according to my detection skill.

Whoa, wait. Couldn't you just farm infinite iron from these golems then?! Well, that would leave a ton of people without jobs, and homeless...

We arrived at the chamber with the five golems. My static bear punches made short work of them, and I was soon headed down the tunnel to slay the mithril golem.

My map updated as I descended, and there it was: the mithril golem, marked on the map. Maybe if I just took this thing out, the rest would go away.

I got to the chamber. Light mana gems had lit the tunnel up until now, but from here on, it was dark. I made a bear light with magic to illuminate the cavern.

There were traces from the battle all over, probably from the bozo rangers' fight. The rock faces were crumbling, holes were gouged in the ground, and I saw evidence that magic had struck the walls.

Even if the bozo rangers were playing it safe, I was still amazed they *hadn't* caused a cave-in. The mithril golem stood in the aftermath of the battle.

It noticed me. It faced me.

Here we go, I guess.

My bears seemed ready to join in since they started walking ahead of me, but I told them to stand back. They let out a soft, sad cry, but I was going to fight the mithril golem alone...and I wasn't going to fight it here.

Powerful magic or a strong bear punch might cause a cave-in here, but that just meant I'd need to move us to a place where I'd be able to take advantage of my OP bear abilities.

I brought out a bear transport gate and touched the gate to open the portal.

Oh, man, but would the mithril golem fit in the bear gate? The gate was wide enough, but this guy was *tall*. Maybe I'd have to really squeeze it in.

I looked over at the mithril golem. It looked back—and then ran at me, footfalls thumping as it came. It was faster than I thought. I guess I just assumed golems were slow.

(Maybe *fast* was overstating it. Really, I meant that it was just faster than I'd expected. It was slow as sludge compared to the black tiger.)

The golem ran at me like a charging bull. And like

a matador, I stepped to the side just in time. I circled around behind it and—*crack!*—got it in the neck with a bear punch. The golem fell headfirst into the bear transport gate. Looked like it had worked out, despite its size.

I followed through the bear gate. Kumayuru and Kumakyu came in after me.

The bear transport gate took us to an open sandy beach along the shore.

We were near Mileela, though we were far enough away from town that nobody would notice. This was where I'd practiced my electricity magic last night. There was plenty of space here compared to the narrow tunnels. Clouds in the blue sky, no ceiling and no walls... I could make full use of my OP bear skills.

I looked at the mithril golem that had fallen headfirst into the sand.

"We can fight each other without worrying about our surroundings," I told the golem. I didn't expect a reply, but it stood up, as if it understood. Well, I'd said *we* wouldn't need to worry, but really, I'd be the only one doing the attacking.

I tried throwing a fireball at the upright mithril golem. It was a direct hit, but the golem stood there like nothing happened. I tried wind magic, earth magic, and ice magic.

All ineffective. I'd expected as much, but really, wasn't it kind of cheating to have your whole body made of mithril? And sure, you might say, "Look who's talking," but I couldn't help but feel that way when my opponent was a mithril golem.

Okay, then how about this?

"Bear cutter."

Visualizing a bear's claws, I fired off bear wind magic. The mithril golem was blown back by the impact, but... seemed unharmed? No, wait, there were three lines on the golem's chest when I looked. I guess I *could* do some damage to it. Maybe if I focused on the same spot, I could take it down.

I tried using another type of bear-type magic as an experiment. Flaming bears emerged from my puppets. I doubted that'd melt the golem, but I needed to check.

The golem blocked the flaming bears with its arm. A normal monster would've been helpless against the bears. Game over. But the flames engulfed the mithril golem's arm and went out just like that.

Dang. But...wait. I took a closer look. Had it melted just a smidge? Maybe I'd be able to slay it if I fired off a whole bunch of flaming bears at it?

Lastly, I tried using the electricity magic I'd learned yesterday.

I gathered electricity around my bear puppet and threw a strong static bear punch at the mithril golem. That sent the golem flying, but it didn't seem like the electric shock had done much.

Ah, man. Guess my new magic wasn't effective against mithril golems.

Still, it felt good actually using my abilities for a change. The golem had become a one-sided punching bag. A punching bag that also happened to be built like an indestructible tank.

The golem stood up, even after my bear punch.

Well, enough experimenting: it was time to finish things. I started running toward the golem and gathered mana in my black bear puppet.

I weaved as I got in close, dodging the arm it brought down to block me, getting under its chest. Then, with the power of wind behind me, I struck it with a bear uppercut.

The golem soared into the air from the impact. It flew high into the sky. That must've been, what, a thousand meters up? It wasn't like I could actually tell just by looking. I couldn't just look at a plane and use some kind of Bear Distance Detector to tell what altitude it was flying at, or how tall a luxury condo was. What I did know was that there was no way the golem would come out unscathed after a drop from that high. And if you specifically factored in the golem's size, weight, and terminal velocity—well, it was going to have a bad time.

The golem spun as it fell, probably because I'd put a little spin into the bear uppercut. It crashed into the ground with a sound and shockwave like that of an earthquake, swirling the sand up over it. I'd definitely gotten this thing.

Or so I thought. The golem looked like it was starting to stand up.

It was still moving after falling from that height? How tough *was* this thing? Why hadn't the impact destroyed its mana gem?

Okay, no, it was standing but it wasn't doing it easily. It'd lost an arm, and its neck was bent out of shape too. The center of its body was cracked from the impact of the fall and I could see its mana gem through there.

Could I finish things by breaking that?

I ran toward the sluggish golem and threw a static bear punch at the crack where I could see the gem. The electricity ran through the crack and, in seconds, the gem was shattered.

With its mana gem obliterated, the mithril golem went completely silent. Mission complete.

I hoped the golems would stop respawning in the mine after this.

My bears came over to me after the battle was over. "That's that, huh?" I patted their heads and put the pile of mithril golem into my bear storage.

Not the way *I'd* want to go, if I were a gigantic deadly mithril golem, but that's just life sometimes. And hey, I needed a cool mithril knife, you know?

After gathering pieces of golem, I used the bear transport gate to get back to the mines. I put the gate away and looked around. The boss's chamber in a game usually had something lying around, like treasure...or possibly even some *treasure?* (Yes, I did say it twice.)

Maybe the source of the golems was here? Or...what if there was a secret room? I inspected the walls trying to find something. I was convinced I would, but nope. Nothing. Nada.

With nothing else to do, I was about to start heading back when Kumayuru and Kumakyu started digging a hole.

"What is it?" I asked as I went over to my bears. They were digging where the mithril golem had originally stood. That'd been in a blind spot for me. Maybe the mithril golem had been protecting something?

I stepped in between Kumayuru and Kumakyu and found two round, black stones in the hole.

"What are these?" I asked. The bears just tilted their

heads at me. C'mon, they were the ones who found the things and they were clueless?

Anyway. I picked up the stones, which were about as big as my fist, and inspected them, but I wasn't a blacksmith and didn't know all the different kinds of ores.

But I did have a skill for that. I pulled my bear hood down and used Bear Identification.

> **Bearyllium.**
> A mysterious ore.

That was it. That was the whole entry.

Bearyllium. Really? *Really?* Wait, were they making fun of me?

Okay, the god who'd brought me to this world had definitely been involved with naming this stuff. There was no way the rest of the world had named it that. Also, what was a "mysterious ore" even supposed to be? If even the very item description called it mysterious, how was I supposed to know how to use it?

Except...thinking back to that first message I'd gotten from that god, hadn't he said that there would be "*other presents around*" and I should do my best to look for them? Maybe this was one of those. This, uh. *Bearyllium.* Ugh.

Plus, how was I supposed to process or even use a mystery ore? Even a video game would've given me more of a hint.

Complaining about that god wasn't going to change anything, so I thanked my bears instead and gave them some good pets.

They were getting a lot of pets today, actually. Not that they seemed to mind. They deserved plenty of gratitude for all they'd done, and they seemed pretty happy with all the attention, anyway.

158
The Bear Leaves the Mines

BEARYLLIUM, THOUGH?

I didn't have enough info to solve *that* particular mystery yet, and it wasn't going to be a problem anytime soon, probably. I put those weird stones I'd found out of my mind and headed home.

When I climbed up a level, I used my detection skill to check for golems.

What?! No way, they were still there?

I guess all the golems wouldn't just stop functioning after I defeated the mithril golem. What if they were totally unrelated? What a pain. My quest had been to slay all of the golems in the mines, after all.

Doing it all on my own would be a hassle, though. I was considering asking Jaden and the others for help when Kumayuru and Kumakyu came up to me.

"You want to help me out?"

"*Kwoom.*"

Seemed like bearspeak for "Leave it to us."

"Thank you. I'll take you up on that," I said and gave them a hug. "I'll slay the iron golems, so you guys have fun with the rock golems and mud golems. Once it's over, let's meet up at the entrance."

Kumayuru and Kumakyu nodded and started to run down the tunnel.

"You two play nice with each other!"

A distant *"Kwoom!"* echoed.

I let my bears handle the upper levels and went to go slay the iron golems myself. There weren't many forks on this level, so I didn't think it'd take much time. I used my detection skill to figure out my route, then headed off.

The iron golems were nothing compared to the mithril golem. After that, I went up to the next level to help my bears...and detected no golems. Kumayuru and Kumakyu were already waiting at the entrance, huddled together and happy.

"Quick work, guys. Good job," I said, and sent them home with a few more head pats for good measure.

Obviously, I was pretty beat after slaying the mithril golem and cleaning out the golems in the tunnels. I was hoping to go back to the inn so I could turn in early. I attracted a few curious looks on my way from the mines to the inn, but I ignored them and kept going.

When I got back to the inn, Jaden's party and the bozo rangers were there.

"You're late, Yuna," said Jaden.

Mel nodded. "I didn't think you'd have issues, but I was a little worried since you hadn't come back after so long."

I'd been cleaning the inside of the mines for a while, after all. "I was slaying golems, so that kept me."

"They'll be back tomorrow," Senia said bluntly. "Remember?"

"Jaden, there's something I wanted to ask you about that."

"What is it?"

"I killed all of the golems, including the one that was furthest in. Could you check on them tomorrow?"

"Sorry. What did you say?"

"The golems? I killed them all, so..."

"Yuna, you're joking right?" Mel asked.

"I slayed them, but I don't know if they'll revive or not." It would take a day to know, at least.

"You there, pet," snarled Bozo Red, coming over to us with a beer in his hand. "Don't you lie! Are you saying that a pet like you defeated the golem on your own when the five of us couldn't even take it down? Don't make me laugh."

Apparently, he'd been eavesdropping on our conversation.

I'd spent a while sweeping the tunnels after I'd slayed the mithril golem, and it had given me time to practice moderating my electricity magic. Might as well test it out.

I charged my bear puppet slightly and gave Bozo Red a light little touch.

"*Uagh-ha?*" With a strange sound, he fell over.

"Barbould?!"

His companions immediately rushed over to him. Bozo Red was out cold. He was still alive...right? Hmm, maybe I'd tone it down next time. I guess I needed more practice. Okay, yep, he was alive and he'd been rude, so you get what you get.

"Wow, how drunk *was* that guy?" I pointed to the beer in Bozo Red's hand. The beer had spilled, but it was mostly empty. He hadn't lost much...

"There's no way he's that drunk, he barely..."

"But he *is* sleeping it off."

Everyone thought I had done something, but nobody could prove anything. Nobody even knew what I'd done. Bozo Red's companions didn't say anything more and carried their hulking leader back to his room.

As for me, I sat down in an empty seat and ordered a meal from the proprietress.

"Yuna," she said, "did you really not do anything to that man?"

I tilted my head to the side and played innocent.

"Yeah, Yuna didn't do anything. Barbould got drunk and fell over." Mel was the only one who nodded.

"Okay, Yuna, but what did you really mean that thing from earlier?"

"What thing?"

"About the golems."

"Oh, that. You don't have to believe me, but I took them all down, including the one furthest in the back. If they don't revive, I think it's over."

Jaden sighed. "I guess it's true then."

"Looks like we were beaten to the punch," said Mel.

Beaten to the punch? But hadn't they given up last night?

"To tell you the truth, we kind of hit it off with Barbould and the others while we were drinking yesterday. We started discussing whether we could team up to take down that golem in the back. If the kingdom was about to take the credit from all of us anyway, we figured it'd be better to split the reward."

"After that we made plans to slay it the next day..." Senia began.

"...and I went out and did it." Oh. I'd just thought they'd all given up.

"Still, can't believe you took it down."

"Well, I had to try some wild stuff."

"Aww, I wanted to see you fight."

I wouldn't have been able to use the bear transport gate if they'd been with me, though.

"Sorry, Yuna, but could you show us the golem? You must be carrying it, right?"

Hmm, they wouldn't notice it was made from mithril if they saw it up close, right? I reluctantly went outside and took out the mithril golem.

"Whoa. Brutal." The golem was in rough shape.

"You took this thing out even after Barbould's group couldn't defeat it."

"Yep. Bear power's nothing to mess with."

"Bear power is really *this* strong?"

As Jaden leaned in to inspect it more closely, the proprietress's voice rang out from inside the inn. The food was ready.

"Coming!" I stashed away the mithril golem. I hadn't wanted them to take a closer look, so this was great timing. I went inside, pretending like I was really looking forward to the meal. Behind me, the party talked on...

"If Yuna defeated the golem, maybe there's been a change in the state of the mines."

"That's right. We'll check on it tomorrow."

"We were planning on going with Barbould's group anyway."

After eating, I went back to my room and visited the place I'd fought the mithril golem with my bear transport gate. I wanted to sleep, but I couldn't leave the gate there forever.

It was dark at the beach. I'd thought the same thing yesterday, but the ocean at night was eerily quiet. I could only hear the crashing waves, could only see by starlight.

Still, I was glad that my movements were obscured by the darkness. Good thing I was wearing black too, even if that just made me look like a huge black bear. I got to my gate on the beach and headed to my bear house in Mileela like a bear-shaped assassin cloaked in midnight.

Once I got to my Mileela house, I used the gate there to head back to my room at the inn. I changed into my white bear outfit and dove into bed, and that was that.

Oh, and of course I summoned my bears in cub form for safety and all. And *then* I was out like a light.

The next day, Jaden's party and the Bozo Rangers headed to the mines. They also invited me, but I pretended to be tired from the day before and stayed behind.

Incidentally, Bozo Red didn't remember what happened yesterday. Even he thought he'd gotten black-out drunk and passed out. I was sure glad he was too much of a bozo to realize otherwise.

I finished breakfast, returned to my room, and plopped onto bed to fall back asleep. Ahh...finally, a day to relax. Fina seemed to be having fun in the capital too.

I'd asked Ellelaura to take Fina sightseeing at the castle. Princess Flora had latched onto me last time, so we hadn't actually been able to see the inside of the castle. When I checked in with Fina over the bear phone, I found out she'd worn beautiful clothes, gone to the castle, and seen the garden. And to think I'd worried about her.

I'd asked Shia to show her around the capital if they had time too. Since I'd brought Fina into this mess, I needed to make sure she at least enjoyed herself.

I woke up a bit late from my nap and went to ask about lunch when Jaden's party and the Bozo Rangers came back.

"That was quick," I said as I sipped my soup.

"Yeah. There wasn't a single golem, so we just walked around and just came back."

"I can't believe it," muttered Bozo Red.. "Not even *one?*"

Had the golems been caused by the mithril golem? Or was it the bearyllium? No way to know right now, but they probably weren't coming back.

"Did this pet of yours really take out that golem by herself?" Bozo Red looked down at me.

Pet? Again? Had he forgotten about the electricity? I guess he had, but I could reacquaint him...

"It was gone. You saw it with your own eyes."

"And you think that's enough to prove your *pet* took down a golem that five of us couldn't handle?"

"How many times do I have to explain Yuna to you?"

"Ha! Are you going to tell me about tiger wolves, black vipers, and goblin kings again? Load of bull is what that is."

Mel sighed. "He has a point. It's a little hard to swallow for most people." When I looked around, it wasn't just Mel. Everyone was nodding. "But Yuna went to the mines alone yesterday, and now the golems are gone. You can't pretend that isn't true."

"I guess..." Bozo Red sank into his chair and sulked.

My bear garb probably didn't inspire much confidence. "So, Jaden, is the quest done now?" If it was, I'd head back right away, since Fina was waiting.

"For now, we'll give a report to the person in charge of the miners. We'll discuss what to do from there."

Oh, yeah, I guess there would be someone in charge of the miners. I'd forgotten all about them, thinking I could just head back to the capital and report to the people there.

"Can you give the report yourself, Yuna?"

"That's such a drag. Could you handle it for me, Jaden?"

Jaden gave me a look at that. Seemed to think it over. Looked over at Bozo Red. "I guess I can give the report. Come with me, Barbould."

Oh, nice—Jaden actually listened to me. What a good guy. I was pretty grateful.

"Why do *I* have to go?" Red Bozo groaned.

"They would probably believe us more if you all were there too."

"Shouldn't you bring along your pet—considering she supposedly killed them all entirely by herself?"

"You think if she went over there and told them she did, they'd believe it?"

Bozo Red gave me a long look. "Guess not."

"So come along now"

"Guess I have no choice."

Wait, was Jaden badmouthing me too in a subtle way? Or was it my imagination?

114

Whatever. I'd forgive him *this* time, since he was making that report for me. Next time, I might get him with a bear punch too.

Jaden's party and the bozo rangers headed to the leader of the mines to give the report. I waited around, trying to decide whether to head home.

I ended up napping with cubified Kumayuru and Kumakyu until Jaden and the others returned. As I lazed around, there was a commotion outside my room. When I opened the window and looked, Jaden's party and the Bozo Rangers were surrounded by townspeople.

The people showered them with thanks. Jaden's party looked kind of bothered by it, but the Bozo Rangers were eating it up.

I wondered what had happened.

Jaden and the others got into the inn even while they were still being thanked by the townspeople. The townspeople didn't follow them inside at least.

I dismissed Kumayuru and Kumakyu and headed to the first-floor dining room. "Did something happen?"

"Oh, uh, Yuna..."

"Uh. We ended up getting the credit for defeating the golems at the mines."

They walked me through what had happened.

First thing in the morning, the nine of them were witnessed going to the mines.

Then the nine of them were seen returning safely.

Then all nine of them were seen reporting to the leader of the mines.

The leader of the mines had thanked them, the story spread that the golems weren't appearing anymore, and... yep, I got the gist of it.

"They thought we had defeated the golems," said Jaden, "no matter what we said."

Senia glared at the Bozos. "You can blame those idiots for waving."

"Shut your trap. All we did was wave 'cause people were thanking us."

"*Anyway.* We tried to explain that you'd slain it, Yuna."

"...But no one would listen to us."

"Sorry." Jaden bowed his head.

Hmm. This...actually worked out well for me, though. I didn't want to be surrounded like Jaden and the others had been, and I didn't want the fame, so what was the problem? All I wanted was credit from the guild. So I told them as much.

"Of course. We'll report that properly to the guild. That's okay with you too, right, Barbould?"

Bozo Red nodded. "Obviously. We're not petty enough to take credit for someone else's achievements."

"Sure, says the one waving earlier."

"They were calling out to me, so I just waved," said Bozo Red blandly.

I didn't have any issue with Jaden's party getting credit for the slaying. Besides, I think hearing that they defeated it would make the townspeople feel better than hearing it was me, and I was fine with that.

Now the quest was complete and I could head back to Fina, and I told them so.

"That's fine," said Jaden, "but we're going to keep an eye on the situation for a while."

"The situation...?"

"This is the first time the golems haven't reappeared after a single day, but we don't know what will happen tomorrow or the day after."

"Right. We're going to stay for five days."

"Huh?" Five whole days...but Fina was waiting for me...

"But you can head back, Yuna."

(Oh, good. No way could I leave Fina with Ellelaura for five more days.)

"If you're going to the capital ahead of us, could you report back to the Adventurer Guild for us?"

"Sure," I said, "but what happens if the golems reappear?"

"We'll leave it to the kingdom then. If that golem revives just like that, I think we'll just throw up our hands and give up." Jaden actually raised his hands.

"Got it. In that case, I'll head back to the capital tomorrow."

It was time to rescue the imprisoned princess.

159
The Bear Returns
to the Royal Capital

I SUMMONED BOTH KUMAYURU AND KUMAKYU and returned to the capital, switching between them as I went. I returned Kumakyu and walked through the capital gate. The gate guards gave me weird looks, but I ignored them.

Crowds kept muttering about this bear passing by. I retreated deep into my hood and sped up, making a beeline for the Adventurer Guild.

When I entered the guild, a bunch of the adventurers looked at me all at once, but no one picked a fight. I guess Sanya's talking-to the other day had been effective. I went to an open reception desk to get the guild master. It seemed like I was on my way to becoming famous, since the receptionist immediately went to call for Sanya when she noticed me.

"Yuna!"

An inner door opened and Sanya came over.

"I'm back," I answered, raising a bear puppet.

I thought we would talk here, but she took me to the guild master's office. I sat in a chair and one of the staff members brought in some drinks. Made me feel like a fancy CEO or something.

"Well, then, what do you have for me?"

I told her that the golems had stopped reviving after I defeated the one furthest in. I explained that Jaden and the others were going to stick around for five days to make absolutely sure the golems weren't coming back.

"You can get the details from Jaden and the others later."

"Excellent. If the golem outbreak really is over after this, we won't need to send the soldiers. That really helps, Yuna...thank you."

"But we still don't know for sure."

"True. Since the quest isn't over until we get the detailed report from Jaden's party, would you mind waiting a few days longer for your reward?"

"Do I have to come back here?"

"No, I can contact Crimonia and you can pick it up there."

"Are you sure?"

"It's the least we can do."

I wasn't about to say no. "Cool. I'll head home, then." Had to get back to Princess Fina, after all.

Sanya stopped me as I stood up. "Hey, Yuna, why not live in the capital instead of Crimonia? It'd make me happy if you were here."

Where did that come from? "Thanks, but I don't think so."

I'd gotten comfortable in Crimonia. People had stopped ogling me, and I didn't get in fights with adventurers. On top of that, my shop was there and there were no benefits to living in the capital. Actually, the increased workload would be awful. Most importantly, since I had a bear transport gate in the capital, I could come by anytime. I didn't have to live here at all.

"That's too bad."

"I can still come by every once in a while to hang out, though."

With my report to the Adventurer Guild turned in, I headed to Ellelaura's estate. When I got there, Fina came running over wearing these lovely clothes.

"I'm back, Fina."

"Yunaaaaaa!" She latched onto my belly. I caught her against my paunch—that is, the bear onesie's paunch. Not mine. I'm not the bear.

"Fina, you look so cute."

She was wearing these cutesy, frilly clothes. She kind of looked like a little well-to-do lady. It was great.

"Not nearly as cute as your bear clothes, Yuna. Besides," she added, "Lady Ellelaura *forced* me to wear this!"

Okay, sure, you could describe both as cute, but Fina's outfit and my outfit were totally different *kinds* of cute. I bet any girl would rather be called cute for wearing nice clothes than for putting on a bear onesie. Fina puffed up her cheeks when she spoke, which made her even cuter— classic cutie hours for Fina today.

I was glad she seemed to be doing fine. If anything terrible had happened, I wouldn't have been able to face Tiermina.

"Welcome back, Yuna," said Ellelaura, coming over from where Fina had. "Is the situation at the mines over?"

"It's over. We just have to wait and see what happens, so I decided to come home."

"Thanks for the hard work. Would you kindly tell me the details? I've got a meal prepared."

Fina and I took a bath together before the meal.

"Did you have fun in the capital while I was gone, Fina?" I asked while washing her back, but Fina didn't respond. Not even a nod or shake of her head.

Had it not been fun for her?

"Yuna, it was tough while you were gone. Lady Ellelaura and Surilina forced me to wear nice clothes every single day..." she answered, pouting.

Wait... she *had* said that Ellelaura had made her change into nicer clothes during our phone call. She also said she'd gone to the castle and seen the king, and that it'd been a lot to handle. Maybe I'd taken it the wrong way.

"Is it so bad to wear nice clothes?"

Fina shook her head slightly. "It wasn't bad, but I was worried I'd make them dirty. The clothes are so expensive. I wouldn't even be able to pay them back."

"Ellelaura wouldn't make you pay her back even if you did make them dirty. If she even tried, I'd give her a talking-to and pay for them myself. Besides, I don't think even *you* really believe Ellelaura is the type to make you repay her."

Fina's expression softened. "Um. Yeah, she *is* pretty nice..."

"Sorry this is how things turned out," I apologized as I scrubbed at her slender back. We'd come all this way for a mithril knife, and I'd really dragged Fina into a mess.

"You were doing your job, Yuna. It's not your fault."

For the rest of the bath, Fina told me all about the good times, the bad times, and how her stomach ached when she met the king. Even through the complaints, I could tell that she enjoyed herself a *little* bit. "Are you listening, Yuna?"

"Mmhm."

"Really? It was really terrible."

"I'm sure."

I gave Fina, who was clearly experiencing a varied spectrum of expressions, a hug.

We got out of the bath and headed to the dining room. Ellelaura and Shia, who had returned from the academy, were already seated.

"Thank you for looking after Fina for me, Shia." I'd asked Shia to show Fina around the capital.

"Not at all. Fina is such a good girl, so it wasn't a problem."

"That's not true. I caused all kinds of trouble," Fina insisted, but Shia was smiling.

"Could you give me a report? Even a short one will do."

I told Ellelaura about the mines while I ate. While I explained about Jaden's group and the Bozo Rangers, I tried to make my role seem as small as possible. Of course, I didn't say a word about electricity magic or the bear transport gate.

I was also really vague about the battles themselves.

"A mysterious golem deep in the mines, you say?"

"They stopped appearing the day after I defeated it, so I think everything's good now. The adventurers staying there are going to check just in case."

"We can't say it's safe after a single day, but yes—the situation seems under control based on what you've said. Thank you, Yuna. Deploying the kingdom's soldiers would've caused all sorts of problems. You've really helped me out."

"Were the golems strong, Yuna?" asked Shia.

"I don't know about strong, but it was hard to fight them in the tunnels. If I used too much power, the tunnel would've caved in. And I couldn't use fire-based magic since it was too cramped."

Shia blinked. "I can understand why the cave-in would be an issue, but I didn't know you couldn't even use fire magic."

Yeah, the low oxygen would make the fire ineffective *and* would've probably suffocated us.

"How did you end up slaying it, Yuna?" she asked.

"That's a secret."

"What? Oh, please tell me."

Nope. Electricity magic and the bear transport gate were top-secret information.

With the meal and my report over, I started to head

back to my room, but Ellelaura stopped me. "Wait a minute. Are you going to head home tomorrow?"

"I need to get Fina back to her parents. I bet they're worried." Ellelaura gave Surilina a signal, and with a quick nod she left. "In that case, I'll give you your reward today."

"My reward? I can get the reward at the Adventurer Guild in Crimonia."

"Not that. Did you forget? I'm giving you a mithril knife."

Oh, right. But now that I had the mithril golem, I didn't need one from her.

Ellelaura's lip curled curiously. "You do need one, don't you?"

Was she psychic?! I shook my head.

"You sound quite certain, Yuna."

While I evaded Ellelaura's suspicions, Surilina returned and handed her something bound tightly in cloth. Ellelaura placed the bundle she received on top of the table, untied the string that bound it, and pulled a beautiful, ornately decorated knife from the cloth.

She presented it to me. "Here you go, Yuna."

The knife seemed very expensive. Its handle and scabbard decorations were finely crafted. This was no butchering knife. "What is this? Why is it so beautiful?"

"I promised you a knife for a reward, didn't I?"

"This wasn't made for butchering carcasses, was it?"

"No. It has other uses."

"And it wasn't made for fighting, either?"

"It isn't, but it *is* actually mithril, so it has a good blade."

Ellelaura drew the knife from the scabbard. The blade was also beautiful. It looked like something a girl might carry for self-defense, but something felt off. What kind of dark stuff was this knife *for?!* Rituals? Suicide? Ritual suicide?!

"I don't need it."

"But why? It's your reward."

"And I don't plan to off myself."

"It's not like that. It's for self-defense."

I guess it really *was* for self-defense. Oops.

"But even though it *is* for self-defense," she continued, "it's *not* for fighting others."

I tilted my head to the side. A knife you couldn't fight people with?

"The knife has the Fochrosé family coat of arms set in it. I thought this could show that you are supported by the Fochrosé family. That's a name with power. If you got caught up in something, you should show off this knife. Troublemakers might well back down at the sight of it. If they don't...kindly tell me about them."

Maybe that would be handy. It was kind of like a seal.

I got mixed up in an awful lot of trouble because of my bear onesie, after all.

"Large merchants and others know the Fochrosé family coat of arms," she said, "so it should be effective with the Trade Guild as well. If you run into trouble, show it off. But be careful using it outside the capital—the further you go, the fewer the people who will recognize it."

Travelers did come to my shop sometimes. Was that what she meant? "Just use it whenever you need."

"I don't think I will." There's that old saying—everything comes at a cost. Using the crest felt like it came with a cost too, and I preferred to know those numbers up front.

Ellelaura presented the knife to me a second time.

"Okay, but...what if I use the knife for nefarious purposes?"

Ellelaura laughed like I was joking. "You're so funny. In what world could a person who took care of an orphanage, who went to slay a black viper to save a small boy, and who dug a tunnel without compensation and handed it over for others to use, use this knife for—what was your word—*nefarious* purposes?"

She stretched out her arm and poked my cheek.

"Maybe I had ulterior motives and was scheming something."

"Oh? Then perhaps some questioning is in order." Ellelaura turned her gaze to Fina, who had been listening silently.

"Fina, is Yuna a bad person?"

"Yuna is a very nice person. If she hadn't been there, my mom and I would have died. The orphans wouldn't be doing well, and I heard from my dad that she killed the black viper for free too. Yuna's kind and strong, and she would never do anything bad. In fact..."

Ellelaura nodded along in agreement.

"I understand, Fina. You don't have to say more than that. You're embarrassing me."

"But I haven't even said half of the good things about you."

"Fina. Please." It'd get too embarrassing if she said more. As a shut-in who wasn't used to praise, I just didn't know how to handle it. I looked at the knife in front of me again.

"If I take it, you can't say I'm one of your servants though."

"I would never."

I put the knife in the mouth of my white bear puppet and it went right into my bear storage.

160
The Bear Goes to the Capital Blacksmith

THE NEXT DAY after I finished my breakfast, I went to the front of the estate to give Shia and Ellelaura my farewells.

"Yuna, please visit next time you come to the capital. You can come anytime too, Fina."

"Yeah, I'll stop by."

"Thanks for everything, Lady Shia."

"Thank you, Yuna. There are still some places in the castle I haven't shown Fina. Next time, maybe we won't be interrupted by any busybodies."

"Okay," Fina responded, but she looked troubled. Had the king really been that terrible to her? Poor thing. I had to protect her next time we went to the castle.

We watched Shia and Ellelaura head out from in front of the estate as they went to the academy and to the castle for work, respectively. From there, Fina and I left for Ghazal's blacksmith shop in the capital.

Fina held onto my bear puppet as we started to walk.

Maybe she'd been lonely after getting split up for a while. I let her hold my hand—not like I had any reason to shake her off, you know?

"Are we still going home, Yuna?" Fina asked me as we walked in a direction that wasn't toward the bear house.

"I wanted to stop by Ghazal's place once before we head back."

I wanted to ask Ghazal something, and there was also the mithril knife. I had some mithril now after slaying that golem.

With Fina holding my hand as we walked, we arrived at Ghazal's blacksmith shop.

"Pardon us. Is Ghazal here?" I called inside.

Ghazal came out from inside. " I was wondering who it was, and here I find you, strange-looking lass."

"Good morning."

"What's brought you at this godforsaken early hour?"

It wasn't *that* early. Didn't a lot of people work right now? "I guess I came to let you know the golem situation at the mines is resolved. Ore should start coming over before too long."

"You don't mean—was that your doing?"

"I helped a little."

I gave him a simple summary of what happened at the mines. "A mithril golem," he said finally. "I can't believe it. And for you to be the one that took it down!"

It wasn't *that* surprising, but I let him have this. "Anyway, I thought I could order a mithril knife from you with the materials from the golem. Can you do it?"

"You'd be best served asking Gold. Since he lives in the same city, I think that'd be more convenient."

"I was just curious. But from what you said, wouldn't making a mithril weapon take a while?"

"Aye, working with mithril is tricky."

"Right. So I thought I could order them from both you and Gold." I was thinking of making two knives for butchering and two knives for fighting.

"I understand why, but you're living in Crimonia. Far less hassle for you to go to Gold, I'd say, with the travel time between here and there."

"That's okay. I have a way to get here right away." Gotta love that bear transport gate.

"I see. If you're sure, you'll hear no qualms from me."

"Thank you. In that case, I'll pull out the mithril golem."

I took the crumpled mithril golem out of my bear storage and placed it in the shop's passageway.

It just barely fit.

"This is the beast?" Ghazal approached the collapsed golem to check it out. He held an arm and a piece of the body and inspected them. He looked serious. Ghazal looked at the destroyed sections of the golem. Then he said something unexpected.

"What is this...this *knock-off*?"

"Knock-what?" I tilted my head, puzzled.

"Exactly! This is a mithril golem, and it isn't a mithril golem."

"Um."

Ghazal showed me a piece of the mithril golem he was holding. "Here and here, the color of the cross section is different." He pointed at a cross-section with his thick finger. He was right—the color really *was* different. "The exterior is mithril, but the inside is iron."

"What, seriously?!"

"I'm not lying to you. If you returned to Crimonia, Gold would also verify this."

I didn't think he was lying, but...the inner metal of the golem was iron? I guess "knock-off" made some sense, then...

"But there is mithril in it, right?"

"About half of it, or maybe a third."

Well, if that god really had set up this golem then god was a real scrooge. The outside was mithril but the inside was iron? Wasn't that like plating? It was like fighting a gold golem and finding out it was just gilded. What a rip-off.

"You want me to make you a butchering knife, you said?"

"That is what I wanted, but can you make two fighting knives?"

"Two of them? For both you and the girl?"

"No, no. Both would be for me. I want one for each hand."

I'd started wanting knives after seeing the way Senia fought. It was cool, seeing her slay iron golems while dual-wielding.

"Two-weapon fighting then?"

"Yeah."

"Fair enough. You ordered them, and so that's that. Okay, hold out your hands."

I held out my hands just as he said, bear puppets at the ready.

"Are you meanin' to make a fool of me? I told you to show me your *hands* 'cause I want to know their size and shape. I need to make knives suited for them."

"But I hold knives with these gloves." I opened and closed the mouths of my puppets.

"You can do that later. Take off those weird gloves and show me yer hands, lass."

Jeez, fine. I took off my bear puppets and showed him my hands.

"Hm. Very tiny." Ghazal touched my palms. It felt a little weird. "And they're soft. Are you really going to fight holding knives with these hands?"

"I mainly use magic, but yeah."

"Then I guess it's fine. But don't come crying to me if you don't train up and get a little bloody with those baby hands of yours. Well, I got the size of your hands. Next, show me again with those strange gloves."

I equipped my bear puppets. Ghazal put his hand in the mouths of my bears and checked my palms. "Good material."

"You can tell?"

He nodded. "*Hrm.* All right, I've mostly got it. So, in a hurry, are you?"

"I'm not really in a rush. It's fine if you take your time." I asked roughly what day they would be complete, and if it would be okay if I returned around then.

"Ah, but what type of mithril are we going with? From what you said, maybe the mana type?"

"Type of mithril?" I tilted my head.

"You were going to make a mithril weapon without even knowing about mithril types?"

I couldn't help it—mithril weapons hadn't *had* types

in my game. Ghazal gave an explanation to me, since I had no clue.

"First off, you can draw out the pure strength of the mithril and focus on the blade's sharpness. This is called the mithril-specialized type. It's generally used by people who can't use magic. For the other type, you can mix the mithril with magic potions and supplement it with mana. That's the mana type. These are used by people who can use magic. Since the mana-type mithril is mixed with other materials, it's not as sturdy, but you can harden it by supplementing it with mana."

"And everyone has some mana, right?" If they didn't, then they couldn't illuminate light mana gems or get water from water mana gems.

"It's not the same. If you haven't mastered magic to a certain degree, you can't use mana-type mithril."

So you needed a *lot* of mana to use mana-type mithril.

"Okay. Which one should I go with, do you think?"

"Depends on the user. Typically, when a mithril-specialized weapon clashes with a wielder's mana type, the specialized mithril wins...but if the weapon is made from mana-type mithril, imbued with mana, its strength changes to match the user. If you can't use magic, then go with the specialized type. If you have confidence in your mana, go with the mana type."

Ghazal continued with his detailed explanation. I'd had no idea these distinctions even existed. In that case, I would go with...

"Mana-type mithril knives, please."

"Then I'll get you two mithril knives." Ghazal took part of the mithril golem. It was only a piece, but it seemed heavy, and yet he lifted it without issue. Was that a dwarf thing? "I'll return any leftovers."

"So how much will it cost?"

"Ah, yes. Since you provided your own mithril, about..." He listed off a few figures.

I didn't know market rate, but it sounded all right to me. I didn't think Ghazal was trying to take advantage of me or anything.

"Good. Then you can pay when you pick up the knives."

"Okay, I'll pay next time I come."

With the discussion about payment over, I thought back to the iron golems. "Oh right. Would you like a souvenir?"

I put the mithril golem leftovers away in my bear storage and pulled out an iron golem I had defeated with an electric bear punch. The creature towered in the passage.

"What's that thing?"

Ghazal was shocked when he saw the iron golem. Well, I guess it would be scary to see a pristine iron golem pop up out of nowhere.

"It's an iron golem. I thought it might really tie the place together. If it was standing in the entrance, wouldn't that really fit your aesthetic?"

"Do you want to scare my customers away?!"

"I just thought it was a good idea. If the golem was holding a sword and shield, I think it would really draw the eye; be good advertising."

"So what, it's supposed to be my door-keep?" Ghazal was astounded. "Besides, I can't accept something this expensive for free."

"It's fine. I have a lot of them."

I didn't have many uses for the iron golems. I could stand to lose one.

"You have a *lot* of *golems*? What *are* you? Gold said in his letter that despite your appearances, you're an excellent adventurer and I should lend you a hand."

"I'm just a C-Rank adventurer."

"You're *just* a C-Rank? And people believe that?" Ghazal looked at my bear outfit dubiously. "All right. I'll take the iron golem as payment for the mithril knives. I'll provide maintenance for those knives free of charge."

"I'll pay the fee."

"Don't need it. But I'll have you know that if that *thing* gets in the way of business, I'm getting rid of it."

"In that case, I'll put it in the corner of the shop." I

strained a little with my bear puppets and moved the iron golem to the corner. "Shouldn't get in the way here."

I looked over my shoulder. Fina and Ghazal stared at me in wonder.

"What is it?"

"Yuna..."

"You're amazingly strong despite those soft hands of yours."

Oh, duh. I suppose frail girls couldn't normally lift iron golems.

"Well, uh," said Ghazal, "I'll get right to it. You can come to pick them up when they're done."

As I went to leave the store, I remembered something. "Oh, right. Can I show you something, Ghazal?"

"What is it?"

I took out the Bearyllium I'd obtained after slaying the mithril golem from my bear storage. "Do you know what kind of stone this is?"

I handed the Bearyllium over to Ghazal, who took it and inspected it closely. Just in case, I kept the name Bearyllium to myself. If no one knew it by that name, I didn't want people thinking I'd named it myself.

Ghazal looked at the Bearyllium from different angles before finally shaking his head. "As far as I know, I've never seen it before."

Even a dwarf didn't recognize this stuff? Exactly what *was* Bearyllium? "It dropped where I defeated the mithril golem."

More accurately, it had been buried.

"I see it's no ordinary stone, but I know nothing more about it. Maybe my master would know."

"Your master?"

"Yes, back in my hometown. Not someone I could consult immediately."

"Where's your hometown, Ghazal?"

"A town near the mines where dwarves have gathered. I studied my master's blacksmithing technique there."

"A town where dwarves have gathered? Really? Oooh, is it far?" A dwarven town, like in a fantasy. I *had* to go there.

"It's quite the journey, yes."

"Can you tell me where it is?"

"Do you want to go?"

"Someday, yeah."

I had to visit the dwarf town—oh, and elven country, too. I wondered if Sanya would tell me where that was? My excitement was growing by the minute.

"If you really do go, I'll write you a letter of introduction for my master."

"Really?! Yes, please."

"In that case, I'll have that ready when you come to get your knives."

"Thank you."

Dwarf town. There was a *dwarf town!*

161
The Bear Hears a Damsel in Distress

AFTER ORDERING knives from Ghazal, I took the opportunity to quickly check off a task that Morin had asked me to do. "Fina, is it okay if I make another stop somewhere?"

"Where are we going?"

"Morin asked me to check on her shop if we were going to the capital."

To check if it was intact, more or less. Her husband had left it behind, so it was important to her to know. Maybe she wanted to return to it in the future? If so, I wouldn't stop her, though I kind of hoped she'd wait until the kids were grown and the shop was taken care of...and I did think she'd want to wait for that too.

We got to Morin's shop. It was small, but it brought back memories. I'd bought Morin's bread here and saved

Morin and Karin when they'd been attacked. If that hadn't happened, I would've never met those two, and they would never have come to Crimonia.

Huh. There wasn't even any graffiti on the old shop. In my original world, someone would've tagged the shutters or something.

"Yuna, who's that out front?"

Hm? There was a girl sitting in front of the store, hugging her knees. I wonder who this was? Maybe she was feeling sad that she couldn't buy Morin's bread? But it'd been so long since the store had closed...

I was curious, so I decided to talk to her. Real bummer if she thought the place was open.

"What are you doing sitting in a place like this?"

When I addressed her, the girl raised her head. She seemed about the same age as me, with light-brown hair just beyond shoulder-length. "Bear?"

I ignored the bear remark and just told her the truth. "If you're trying to get in, the bakery closed down."

"Yeah, I heard. There was some trouble, and the people working here went away."

Was that the impression bystanders had come away with? It was true that there'd been a struggle inside the bakery. And people *had* vanished a few days later. It'd also been right around the time of the king's birthday celebration. Since they disappeared during that commotion, I supposed it was only natural that rumors would abound.

"Where did you go, Auntie Morin?" she said sadly. "If you're safe, let me know..." The girl lowered her head and hugged her knees more tightly. Fina and I exchanged surprised looks at that.

"Um, do you know Morin?" I'd been thinking of just heading out, but I couldn't very well do that now, you know?

"Do you know Auntie Morin?!" The moment I said Morin's name, the girl practically whipped her head up and looked at me. "Do you know where Auntie Morin is? I asked so many people, but no one knew."

I guess Morin didn't tell her neighbors that she was going to Crimonia?

"Morin and her daughter, Karin, opened a new shop in Crimonia."

"Really!?" The girl stood up and firmly grabbed my shoulders.

"Yeah. We just came from Crimonia. We know Morin and Karin."

The girl looked at Fina for confirmation. Fina nodded. "Yeah, they let me eat yummy bread."

"It's true. It's really true. Oh, thank goodness. They're

not dead. When I heard people saying the shop had been destroyed, or that scary men were searching for them, I thought something might have happened..."

The girl sank to the ground as if she couldn't support her own weight.

If she'd only heard bits and pieces of what happened, it was reasonable she'd think they might be dead. I guess no one had been talking about a bear saving them?

"They opened a shop in Crimonia, then. When my uncle died, I wondered what would happen...but that's good!"

"So you do know Morin, right?" Just to get clarification, you know.

"Mmhm! Auntie Morin, she's my dad's little sister."

I could see the family resemblance, now. Still...wow. Did Morin not even tell her family that she was going to Crimonia? She seemed like someone who'd be more considerate than that...right?

"Umm, thank you very much for telling me," the girl said, grasping my bear puppet. "You said Crimonia? Do I have enough money to go there?"

She popped open her purse and began counting the change within.

"Oh, I don't know...and then there's today's stay at the

inn. I was hoping Auntie Morin would look after me, so I don't have much." The girl gave her purse a forlorn look. "I'll need to find work somewhere to save up..."

"Yuna..." Fina tugged at my clothes. *I know*. I didn't know why she had to meet Morin, but I wasn't about to leave somebody's family behind. I wouldn't be able to face Morin again if something happened to the girl.

I took some money out of my bear storage and held it out to the girl.

"Huh?"

"You can use this." It was the same amount, enough to cover a safe carriage to Crimonia, that I'd given to Morin and Karin before.

The girl looked at the money. The girl looked back at me. "Umm?"

"This should pay for a carriage to Crimonia."

The girl just stared at the money and didn't really move to accept it. It started annoying me, so I grabbed the girl's hand and stuffed the money in it.

"But, um, I—I can't accept money from a girl I never even met. I'm already in your debt for you telling me where Auntie Morin is. And you really *can't* just hand out money to people you don't know. Didn't your mom and dad ever teach you that?"

This girl was my age and treating me like a child? Come on. "You're not a stranger, not really. I know Morin, and I'm not going to abandon her family. I mean, if she found out, I wouldn't be able to face her again. Don't worry about the money. If it really bothers you, you can pay me back when we're *both* back in Crimonia."

The girl thought and then tightly held onto the money in her hand.

"Thank you. I'll definitely repay you. Will you tell me where your house is?"

"You'll know it when you see it. Head to where Morin is first. She's at a bakery called the Bear's Lounge. Don't forget that."

"Could you at least tell me your name?"

"They call me Yuna. Morin will know me if you ask her."

"I'm Nerin. Thank you, Yuna. I'll definitely return the money."

And with that, Fina and I parted ways with Morin's niece, Nerin. It had never occurred to me that I might meet a relative of Morin's in front of her bakery. Maybe Nerin would end up working at the shop.

"Yuna? Why didn't you tell her Morin was working at *your* shop?"

"Thought it'd be more interesting that way."

"You're so mean, Yuna."

Maybe that was the reason. Or maybe, deep down, I considered the shop more Morin's than mine.

After leaving Nerin, we ate a meal at a food stand and returned to Crimonia.

"We're finally back."

It'd been a while since I'd been back in my primary home in Crimonia. I'd originally thought we'd be gone for a day, not several. I guess I could think of the whole thing in terms of a special event in the MMO, complete with it being *much* longer than I'd expect it to be.

Still, I was happy that I'd been able to get mithril... even if I'd caused some trouble for Fina.

"What are you going to do today, Yuna?" Fina asked.

Since we'd stopped to buy and eat some snacks at food stalls in the capital first, it was a little past lunchtime now. "You're tired too, aren't you? I was going to take you home to rest up."

She was just ten. She had to be beat after staying out for a few days. Besides, I wanted some rest too.

But Fina rejected my offer. "I'll be fine going home on my own."

"But...I need to say hi to Tiermina."

"That's okay. My mom knows you'd like to say hi, even if you're tired."

"Really? In that case, how about you come by my house tomorrow morning with Shuri?"

"With Shuri?" Fina tilted her head to the side like I'd said something strange.

"Yeah, both of you."

"Okay. I'll come with Shuri tomorrow morning."

"And do say hi to Tiermina for me, all right?"

Fina nodded. "I know it was all kind of crazy, but thank you for taking me to the capital. I felt kinda like I was dead when I met the king, but it was fun."

"Hey, long as you had fun."

"I, uh, didn't really like meeting the king, but I do want to try going with Shuri next time to see the castle garden."

"We'll all go together sometime."

"Uh-huh," Fina answered and left the bear house.

Now that I was alone, there was no way I was going out. Instead, I just relaxed, spending time with Kumayuru and Kumakyu in my room.

162 The Bear Is Scolded by Fina

THE DAY AFTER we returned to Crimonia, Fina brought Shuri over to my bear house. Good kid, Fina—she always kept her promises.

"Good morning, Yuna."

"Morning, Yuna!"

The pair of sisters gave me a friendly greeting.

"Morning to you both. Ready to head out?" They agreed and we left the bear house.

"Tiermina wasn't upset with me?" I asked after a while. I was still a little worried about Fina going home alone yesterday.

"No, it was okay. She wasn't worried because I was with you."

I was glad she trusted me, but was that good parenting? Could I make a joke about that, even?

"Where are we going today, Yuna?" Shuri asked, holding tight to Fina's hand and my bear puppet.

"We're going to Gold's place to make a knife."

"Make a knife?"

She tilted her head a bit. Come to think of it, I hadn't given her an explanation.

"When Fina and I went out together, we got some mithril ore. I'm going to have Gold make a knife with that ore," I explained, summarizing real quick for little Shuri.

"But...why am I here too?"

"We're going to make a butchering knife that will fit your small hands." I held Shuri's small hands, and yeah, they really were teeny.

"But you gave me a knife before."

"It's different from the one we're getting you now."

"A different knife?" Shuri tilted her head to the side again. Well, seven years old was a bit young to understand different kinds of ore.

"It can cut more than that other knife."

Shuri had started showing more interest in learning things recently. When there were animals and monsters to butcher, she would come with Fina to my bear house to watch and lend a hand. If she went to the shop, she'd ask questions about Morin and Anz's cooking. She'd poke her head into the kitchen, read up on things, help

152

Tiermina, and even help take care of the birds at the orphanage. I guess she was at the age where kids were interested in a bit of everything.

Because of that, I'd given her the butchering knife I'd never used while she was watching Fina's work. And yes, I *was* giving a seven-year-old a knife, but Tiermina and Gentz hadn't said anything against it. Back in Japan, I would've gotten in trouble for giving a knife to a child, but in this world, it seemed reasonable for kids to have one in case they came in handy.

Not that she could just carry it on her at all times, of course. I kept it in the storage of my bear house, and Shuri only used it when she was helping Fina with butchering. I didn't know where Shuri would go from here, but maybe she would get a job with the guild like her father Gentz. If so, picking up some butchering skills wasn't the worst idea.

If I did wind up with mithril knives for butchering, *I* wouldn't be using them myself. Best to make one for Shuri too, even if she didn't use it much.

"Yuna, are you going to give Shuri a mithril knife too?"

"Yeah. Didn't I tell you yesterday?"

"You just said to come to your house with Shuri."

"Did I?"

"Yes!" Fina puffed out her cheeks at that. She seemed

mad. "Yuna! This is weird! What is going on in your head?!"

"Why are you getting angry?" It was unusual for Fina to raise her voice like that. I couldn't believe she was angry.

"Do you even know how much a mithril knife costs? I already wasn't sure about whether or not I should accept one, but to just make one for Shuri like it's nothing? I can't even believe it!"

She wasn't just scolding me now. She was...lecturing me? Shuri stared at her older sister in confusion.

"Um, Miss Fina? I don't think this is something to get that mad about."

Hold on, had I just called Fina a "Miss"?

Apparently, she wasn't done lecturing me. "Listen up. Do you know how many months of my mom's salary it would take to buy a single mithril knife? Huh?"

I hadn't even known mithril existed until recently. I had no clue how much it cost. And I wasn't even *from* this world, to boot, so...this felt like an unfair question. But it wasn't like I could just say that, so I tried guessing.

"Umm, about three months?"

Engagement rings cost about three months' salary in Japan, so that had to be about right...roughly. Maybe. Right?

"No! They're not! That! Cheap!" Fina snapped.

I was getting publicly annihilated by a ten-year-old on a street with pedestrian traffic.

"I've been thinking this for a while now, but you have a strange sense of money!"

"I'm sorry."

The conversation was going in a strange direction, but I couldn't exactly point that out to Fina in her current state. I also couldn't deny she was right, especially since there were plenty of examples to support her point that came to mind... All I could do for the moment was hear her out.

I mean, it did surprise me to hear that the price of a mithril knife wasn't even comparable to Tiermina's wages. Was her salary that low? That meant I was going to have to raise it...but that was a topic for another time.

"Please *think* before you act, Yuna!"

"Sorry." I thought she'd get madder if I argued, so I just apologized.

When I did, something tugged my arm. I looked down to see Shuri pulling on it.

"Yuna, I don't need a knife," said Shuri. I guess her sister had frightened her into saying that.

"Okay. Your sister will get mad if I give you one, so...I'll *lend* you one."

I patted Shuri's head.

"*Yunaaaa!*"

"There's no harm in her borrowing one. It's there if she needs it, and if she doesn't, it'll just be in the storehouse."

Fina huffed. "But...!"

"But she can only use it when you're there. Think about it a bit, Fina. Do you think *I* would use a butchering knife, even if I had one?" I thrust out my chest a little when I said that.

I'd thought about giving butchering a shot at some point, but hadn't been able to bring myself to actually do it. I had experience cutting down monsters and animals in battle, so I could slice into the belly of a wolf...but sticking your hands all up in those warm guts? Nope.

Disemboweling animals was a tall order for a modern kid who'd been raised in a city. It wasn't even like I had experience doing it in the game—the game had been merciful enough to just put all the loot right in my item storage without the need for butchering.

"Yuna, aren't you an adventurer?"

I was, but it didn't matter how dumbfounded Fina seemed—I just couldn't do what I couldn't do. Giving me a mithril knife was the equivalent of casting pearls before ursine. I wished I had some kind of butchering skill—like if I could touch a monster and have it instantaneously

156

butcher itself for me? That would be great. But if wishes were horses, beggars would ride.

Fina laughed as she saw me look dejected. "C'mon, Yuna, please don't be that down."

"Fina?"

"If you could butcher animals, I'd be in trouble. Butchering is the only thing I can help you with. Besides, if you could do it, I...don't think we would be here like this together." Fina gave the bear puppet in her hand a squeeze. When I looked down, she looked sad for a moment.

"Huh?"

"I think we're like this now because I could butcher things and you couldn't, when I first met you. So, um, it's good that you can't. Because I'll do it for you," she said, looking up at me.

She wasn't kidding either. The look in her eyes was dead serious.

"Fina..."

"I'll help too," Shuri declared as she grabbed Fina's hands and my bear puppets.

Did they think I'd abandon them if I learned to butcher my own kills? I would never do anything of the sort.

I was already holding their hands with my bear puppets, so I pulled them close in for a hug.

"You sure? Next time I'll slay a whole dragon."

"Yeah! I'll do a great job butchering it."

"I'll work hard too."

I patted their heads. They were such cute sisters.

"But please start taking money seriously."

"I'll work on it," I said, and she just beamed.

163
The Bear Goes to Make a Butchering Knife

HAND IN HAND, the three of us arrived at Gold's blacksmith shop.

"Pardon us," I said, going straight inside. Nelt was usually the one tending shop, but someone else seemed to be filling in for her today—Gold himself, blunt expression and all, polishing the swords that were for sale.

"Gold?"

"Ah, if it isn't Fina, Shuri, and the bear girl!" When he looked at the little girls, his expression softened. He practically turned into a grandpa.

"It's unusual for you to be tending the shop." First time I'd seen it, probably.

"I spent too much time lazing around, so Nelt gave me a good kicking. I'm stuck polishing the merchandise now, heh."

"Where is Nelt?"

"She went out to meet a friend in the area. What's your business here, now? Didn't you head out to the capital?"

"We came here after meeting with Ghazal. Thank you very much for the letter of introduction." I'd thanked Nelt when I received the letter from her, but I still hadn't thanked Gold for writing it.

"To think you got back already too...but I suppose you do have your bear summons." If he could come to a workable answer by himself, I wasn't going to correct him and say it had been the bear transport gate. It looked like he knew Kumayuru and Kumakyu, even though he'd never seen them before. Made sense—word spreads in a small town, they say.

"Was Ghazal doing well?"

"He seemed fine."

"Was he now? Haven't seen him in a while. Maybe I'll go sometime with Nelt to visit," he said fondly, stroking his long beard. "Now then, were you able to get yourself a mithril knife?"

"There were some problems, but we got some mithril ore. I was thinking you could make mithril butchering knives for Fina and Shuri."

"You didn't have Ghazal make them for you?"

"I asked Ghazal to make me knives for fighting, but

I have a lot of ore. When I thought about the maintenance *these* knives would need, I thought I'd ask you. You wouldn't want to do upkeep on knives that someone else made, would you?"

"Bah, why would I care? It's a fine thing, to study the creation of another craftsman. How can you grow your art if you don't learn from other peoples' strengths and polish your skills?"

Know what? That was kind of cool. That was dedication right there.

"That said, bear, do you really want me to make mithril knives for the girls? Do you know how much mithril is worth?"

"I do."

Fina had taught me on the way here. In detail. Loudly.

"As long as you understand. I'll be making a knife for Fina then?"

"And then one for Shuri too, please."

"One more time: You *do* really know how much mithril is worth?" He looked at me with narrowed eyes.

"I do." I knew this wouldn't be something you thoughtlessly handed to a child. "I intend to lend Shuri's knife to her when I think she needs it."

"Is that so? Don't you want a butchering knife for yourself?"

"I wouldn't use one even if you made it."

"So says the adventurer, eh?"

Ugh, was I just going to get this from everyone? I guess most adventurers could butcher things. Oh, well—I had my bear storage, and I had Fina to do my butchering work. I wasn't going to give up on that.

"How much mithril ore do you have?"

"A, uh... golem's worth?"

I pulled out the partially destroyed mithril golem from my bear storage.

"Is all of this pure mithril?"

"Ghazal said it was a knock-off."

"A knock-off?" I explained what Ghazal had told me. Gold listened to my explanation, approached the mithril golem, and examined a piece.

"Ghazal says some interesting things. Iron with a mithril coating. This is my first time seeing a mithril golem; I've never heard of such a thing." He didn't have anything else to say about it. "This should be enough mithril. Did Ghazal take the parts that are missing?"

"Yep. Ghazal took a bit to make my knives."

"As will I." Gold lifted a portion of the mithril golem like it was nothing. Jeez, dwarves were absolute tanks. "When do you need them by?"

"I don't need them particularly quickly, but we'll need Fina's first."

I wasn't really in a rush to get the black tiger butchered. I was just happy that it *could* be butchered.

"Okay. In that case, we're looking at three days for Fina."

"Gotcha. How much will that cost?" I thought the price would be different compared to the fighting knives Ghazal was making for me, but I got an answer I didn't expect.

"No idea. I'll leave that to Nelt."

Ugh, this dwarf was useless. Ghazal took pride in his work too, but he had a handle on the other aspects of his business. Gold only seemed to know the forge. I guess that's why I usually only saw Nelt at the shop.

"Uhh, so then...what should I do for payment?"

"Just ask Nelt!"

I was having second thoughts about the whole leaving-Gold-to-mind-the-shop thing.

After that, in order to make Fina and Shuri's knives, Gold looked at their hands and discussed what material to use for the handles. I didn't follow their conversation. Shuri seemed about as lost as I did, so we just listened, leaving Fina to decide the specifics of the knives.

While I was looking at the weapons inside the store, someone entered.

"Oh, is that you, Yuna?"

"Nelt? Thank goodness. I have something I want to ask you."

"What is it?"

I told her about how I had obtained mithril, how I'd come to order knives for Fina and Shuri, and how the girls were discussing things in the back.

"But Gold doesn't know how much to price them."

"Sorry about that. If the goods are already in the shop, he can sell them. If it's new, though, he's clueless. Still, I can't believe even he would accept a job without setting a price." Nelt let out a weary sigh.

"I trust you two on these things."

"I'm glad to hear that. In that case, I'll give you a bit of a discount."

"Are you sure?"

"Well, I'm glad you're giving that man some work."

What would an artisan be without work? Gold had said as much. "Oh, and I have a souvenir for you."

"A souvenir?"

"I also got this when I got mithril. I was wondering if you would like it to decorate the place." I took out an iron golem and put it in the shop where it wouldn't get in the way.

Nelt jumped a little. She approached the iron golem cautiously to touch it.

"It won't move, will it?"

"It won't."

"It's not damaged anywhere. This is the first time I've seen an iron golem in such good condition. You don't mean to say you're simply giving this to us? Do you know how much the raw iron alone could sell for?"

"I thought you might want to have it hold a sword and shield to decorate the shop. Something like that."

"It would certainly be a waste to melt down an iron golem in such pristine condition, but hmm. Could we bend its arm enough to hold a weapon?" Nelt lightly tapped the golem. It was still in the same pose as when I'd defeated it. "I could try to detach an arm and make the joint movable. Hm, that might work."

She was definitely the wife of a craftsman. But then...if she could do that, I wonder if she could remodel the other golems as well. If she did, I could give them all sorts of poses.

Nelt accepted the iron golem and promised that she would decorate it with a sword and shield. Then, she let me have the mithril knife for free, just like Ghazal had. "It's because you brought your own mithril," she added. "Other than that, it's only his skills you'll need."

Hold on, wasn't I paying *for* the skills? But I wasn't going to say no to Nelt's unending kindness, so I accepted the offer.

As I talked to Nelt, the girls finished up.

"Thank you very much."

"Mmhm! Thank you very much."

Fina and Shuri bowed their heads to Gold.

"You're done?"

"Yes. I think they will be very nice." Fina seemed happy.

"I hope it'll be a nice knife."

"Me too."

We said bye to Nelt and Gold and left the store.

164
The Bear Reunites with Blitz's Group

AFTER I LEFT GOLD'S SHOP, I headed over to Tiermina. I was going to apologize for keeping Fina away from home so long, even if I did technically have permission. Fina said that I didn't need to do that, but I couldn't feel okay till I did.

"I'll let you borrow her anytime, so take her wherever you want," Tiermina told me. She seemed way too comfy about all of this, but I wasn't about to tease her for it. I'd come at this with a serious approach.

"Well, then, I'll keep borrowing her in the future," I said, very seriously.

From the other room, Fina yelled out "Moooom!" (It was pretty great.)

"Now that I think of it, I have a message for you from Anz," Tiermina said.

"From Anz?"

"Someone you know came by the shop, apparently."

"Someone I know...? Did she say who?"

"Not really. That's all she said, so I don't have a clue."

Someone I knew had come by? Who the heck could that have been?

The cheese guy? Zamol, with the potatoes? But if either of them stopped by, they'd go to Morin's shop, and Tiermina would've known them if they had. I thought it over, but I couldn't come up with anything. Thinking about it wasn't getting me anywhere, so I left Fina and the others and went to Anz's shop myself.

I caught sight of Anz's shop ahead of me. The stone bear holding a fish stood out front, promising seafood.

When I passed by the bear, Seno noticed me. "Yuna?" She rushed over, wearing her apron embroidered with a bear. They'd all seemed embarrassed about those bears at first, but now they'd all either gotten used to it or even liked the things.

"Is Anz in?" I asked Seno.

"She is. Aaaaanz! Yuna's here!" she yelled toward the kitchen.

Anz came out of the kitchen, bear apron over her clothes. "Ms. Yuna, where *were* you?"

"I went for a little expedition. I heard from Tiermina that somebody I know stopped by. Who was it?"

"It was Mr. Blitz. I saw him at the shop a few days ago."

"Blitz?"

Blitz was one of the adventurers I'd met in Mileela. He'd helped me get rid of some robbers. Actually, hadn't he said he'd come by once stuff in Mileela settled down?

"He didn't know where you were. When I asked Ms. Tiermina, she said you had gone out with Fina. That's why I asked her to let you know."

"So did you ask Blitz where he's at? Like, the inn he's staying in or something?"

"I didn't ask for the name of his inn, but he did say he was working in town for a while. I think you'll see him if you head to the Adventurer Guild."

If he was gonna come say hi, he could have at least told her which inn he was at. "Thanks, I'll head over to the Guild." He probably wouldn't be there, but maybe Helen knew something.

When I headed into the guild, it was quiet—maybe it was the time of day. Unlike the capital, nobody shot me awkward looks. Even when they did look at me, they'd just be like, "Oh, it's just the bear," and that was that.

I looked around but didn't see Blitz or the others.

"Ms. Yuna, what brings you here at this hour?" Helen

called out from her seat at the reception desk. She looked bored, and I was thinking about asking her anyway, so...

"I heard that an adventurer named Blitz came by recently. Do you know where he is right now?"

"Mr. Blitz?"

"He came from Mileela. He's also got this entourage of three women. One of them is beautiful, one of them is cute, and one of them is way cool. It's very manly-man harem stuff. Probably even makes guys jealous." That seemed accurate enough, yeah?

Helen hesitated. "Um, are you possibly talking about the person...right behind you?"

I whirled around, and yep—there was Blitz, standing tall as ever.

"Been a while." I lifted my bear puppet up in greeting.

"Don't you 'been a while' me. What were you just saying about me?!"

"I thought I was giving a recognizable description of you."

"How is *that* recognizable?"

I looked at the three women behind Blitz. There was a beautiful woman, a cute one, and a cool-looking one right there. "You don't think I was wrong, do you?"

The three of them gave me ambiguous smiles.

"Ha! Yuna, it's been a while."

"Nice to see you again, Rosa. You all look like you're doing great." I looked back at Ran and Glimos, standing next to Rosa.

"Of course we are."

"You're not looking too shabby yourself."

Ran and Glimos were their usual selves.

"Yuna, you didn't come here looking for us, did you?"

"You were the one to stop by Anz's shop. What's the job today?"

"We haven't gotten one," Blitz said bluntly.

"We were sightseeing around the town until just now," said Rosa.

"This place is gigantic," added Ran.

"Then what're you all doing at the Adventurer Guild then?"

"We were thinking of doing a job tomorrow," said Rosa, "so we came by to check out the quests."

"Yeah, before this bear started bad-mouthing me."

"Don't play the victim. I haven't said a bad word about you, Blitz."

"How's that? You said I have an entourage of three women..."

He must've heard the whole thing. "Do you *not*?"

There *really were* three women surrounding Blitz. Blitz looked at them for a moment and finally seemed to get it.

"Then what was that whole thing about me making other guys jealous?"

"Just take a look around."

I pointed to the other adventurers in the place. Blitz turned to look at them, too, and the men just nodded in agreement with what I'd said, rendering him silent.

With the cat firmly holding Blitz's tongue yet again, Rosa took over the conversation. "I asked all kinds of people about you, Yuna. It seems like everyone knows you. They say you even started a fight at the Adventurer Guild."

Nah, I'd only shaken someone off for having a go at me.

"And I can't believe you beat a black viper and a goblin king solo," Ran said.

"Also, we went to the shop you run, too," said Rosa. "It was so busy."

"Yep. We went to eat lunch at the Bear's Lounge. The bread was delicious."

Glimos broke in, her stoic face cracking into a smile. "That bear bread? Pretty cute."

"We went to Anz's shop too," said Rosa. "She gives Deigha a run for his money."

"You already ate there? But I was hoping to treat you..."

Rosa grinned. "I didn't know we could only eat there

once. You might just have to treat us to a second meal."
Because Rosa and the others were C-Rank adventurers, I
thought they'd had more than enough money to afford
it, but a promise was a promise.

"Fair enough. Where do you guys want dinner?"

"Anz's food is great, and that bread was so *good*," said
Rosa.

"I can't choose one," Ran groaned.

They looked tortured.

"You guys helped me out a ton, so I'll treat you to both.
You're going to be in Crimonia for a while, right?"

"That's the plan. We're going to accept some quests
and enjoy the town."

"Then let's go to Anz's shop today. You had the bread
this afternoon, right?"

We decided to eat at Anz's shop for dinner. Even
though it was a little early for a meal, we ended up heading over right away.

KUMA
KUMA
KUMA
BEAR

165
The Bear Makes a Shortcake

I'D FINALLY PERFECTED the devil's food. I scooped up some of the white, finished fluff with my finger, and licked it. "Sweet."

After I'd finished eating with Blitz's group, I saw that there were strawberries for sale in town...and here I was with an irresistible craving for shortcake. After three days of research, I'd finally finished making the fresh cream.

This cream would be expanding my horizons as far as confectionaries were concerned.

I whipped up a sponge cake right away as step one. I cut it in half so it had upper and lower pieces and sandwiched a giant helping of strawberries and cream in between. I spread the cream over the whole thing, then tidily arranged some strawberries on top. I only had the vaguest knowledge of this stuff from my previous world, but it was enough: my strawberry shortcake was complete.

I cut up the cake right away and got it onto a plate, but...compared to the shortcakes I'd seen sold in stores, this thing was a sorry sight. Nonetheless, I attacked it with my fork and wolfed it down.

Yup, delicious. Totally worth it. Was it pro-baker level? Of course not, but it was good enough for an amateur like me.

Still, I couldn't let myself overeat. I wasn't one to put on the pounds, but I still had had to watch my sugar intake. With the bear onesie, people couldn't really tell what my body looked like, but you never know who you'll bathe with. If Fina and Shuri ever said something like, "You've got a soft belly," I don't think I'd ever recover from the shock.

While I was eating my first strawberry shortcake in a long while, someone came by the bear house. Who would barge in right when I was mid-cake?

"Yuna..."

"What's wrong, Fina?" When I opened the door, I found Fina outside. If it'd been Cliff or Milaine, I would've sent them packing, but I couldn't do that to Fina.

"I thought today we were going to pick up the mithril knife from Mr. Gold..."

"Now that you mention it, I guess so." It'd completely slipped my mind during my three-day cake obsession. Oops.

"It was three days, just like he said," said Fina with a truly powerful pout-lecture.

Argh, today wasn't the day for this. I'd just perfected making fresh whipped cream and was in the middle of feasting on my strawberry shortcake. It wasn't like the knife was going to run off on me, but the cake? The cake could spoil. Guess I had the bear storage, but...nope, my top priority right now was stuffing my face with that cake.

"Fina, I made something delicious. Would you eat it with me instead of going to get the knife?" I grabbed Fina's hand as she was standing in the doorway and dragged her into the bear house. I'd gone to all that trouble making the cake; I might as well get Fina's opinion on it.

After I sat Fina down in a chair, I brought the cake out in front of her. I even prepped some milk for her to wash it down with. "What is this?"

"It's a strawberry shortcake. It's good. Take a bite, let me know what you think."

Fina timidly brought the cake up to her mouth. Guess

she was kind of scared of eating something unfamiliar? But after one bite, her eyes shot open wide.

After she took a bit of the cake, the look on Fina's face changed.

"So? How is it?"

"It's delicious!"

Fina ate a second bite, then a third. She was fully invested in polishing off the cake. She was savoring every bite, but she wasn't gonna slow down either. Her face was a mess of cake and cream, capped with a huge smile.

"What's this white stuff?"

"Whipped cream. Basically, I whipped some milk. I used some sugar in it too."

"The strawberries are good too."

Strawberry shortcake was a sure winner. Maybe I'd even try making a cake with a different fruit next time. Before I knew it, the shortcake in front of Fina was gone without a trace.

"So...good?"

"*So* good!" She was on cloud nine...and glancing at the other strawberry shortcake positioned a little away from her. She was usually so mature for her age that it was kind of a relief seeing her actually act like a child.

I silently cut the cake and put it on Fina's plate. Fina looked at the cake and then at me.

"No, you can go ahead."

But she didn't dig in.

"You're not going to eat it?"

"Can I bring it home? I want to let Shuri try."

"Ha! Aww."

"Wh-why are you laughing?! Is it funny?"

I gave Fina a pat on the head, unable to restrain a smile at how much she loved her little sister. She was a great kid—and one who really cared about her family.

"There's still plenty, so don't worry about it. Plus, once I run out of cake, I can just make some more." I cut slices for Shuri and Tiermina, then put them into a basket. "Make sure to ask Shuri and Tiermina what they think too."

I handed the basket to Fina.

"Thank you, Yuna!" With that out of the way, Fina dug into the cake in front of her. After her second slice of the new cake, she thanked me and headed out, homeward bound.

Hm? I kind of felt like I was forgetting something. Maybe it was just my imagination?

A few seconds after Fina left the bear house, she rushed right back.

"Yuna, the knife. We need to go to Mr. Gold to get the knife!"

Oh, right. Both our heads had been too full of cake thoughts to remember that knife.

We headed over to pick up the mithril knife from Mr. Gold. When we got to the shop, the iron golem was standing in front of it...and lookin' slick. The iron golem held a sword and shield. It made me pretty happy, seeing my present to him out on display.

"Whoa. Yuna, this is the golem you fought while I was at Lady Ellelaura's house, isn't it?"

"Yeah. Why?"

"I'm just really glad you got home safe."

It was nice to hear her say that. "Thanks."

After one more look at the iron golem, I headed inside with Fina.

"I've been waiting for you," said Nelt, who was once again stuck tending the shop.

"Is it done?"

"Of course it is. That's the only thing the man is good at, after all," Nelt said as she handed a knife wrapped in cloth to us. Fina took it rather than me.

She pulled off the cloth to reveal a beautiful butchering knife. It didn't have any of the decorations of the knife that Ellelaura had given me, but it was elegant and lovely that way.

Fina slowly unsheathed the knife.

"What do you think?"

She gripped the knife in her tiny hand and looked at the blade tip. "It's very easy to hold. Real nice, and it's very pretty."

She tilted it around to get a look at it from all kinds of angles, held it to the light of the window, and smiled happily. I was getting just the slightest bit of a dangerous vibe.

"Yuna, um! Thank you very much!" Fina turned, fully beaming at me. Seeing how happy she was made the present worth it.

"I'm going to ask you to really get at that butchering with it, though, okay?"

"Yeah. I'll do my best." Fina returned the knife to its sheath and carefully put it away into her item bag. "Thank you very much, Mrs. Nelt. Thank you for making me such a nice knife."

"I'll let my husband know. Bring it by for maintenance if it ever gets dull."

Since the cost of maintenance had been included with the iron golem payment, it'd be free...not that Nelt hadn't already been sharpening her knives out of the kindness of her heart way before then. Even after Fina was in a better situation, what with Tiermina starting to work and getting her new dad, Gentz, they'd apparently turned her down when she offered to pay. They really were a kind old dwarf couple.

"Now then, please stop by in three days for the second one."

"We're in no rush. Take your time."

"Ha! No, it's fine. If I don't make him work, Gold will slack off."

"In that case, if you could do it at a moderate pace...?"

I thanked Nelt and left the shop.

Good, that was out of the way. Now, to business: more cake!

Oh...butchering the black tiger? Yeah, we could do that later. Cake time.

166
The Bear Gets the Black Tiger Butchered

FINA STARTED BUTCHERING the black tiger the next morning.

I pulled the black tiger out onto the giant table. The monster was covered in jet-black fur. Obviously, it was larger than a wolf. Even tigerwolves would take a look at this thing and skulk away.

Fina pulled out the mithril knife that Gold had made for her, took a deep breath, and slowly slid it into the black tiger's flesh. I suppose it was a mithril knife after all—it sliced easily through the black tiger's pelt, which an iron knife hadn't been able to do.

Of course, it wouldn't cut through a *living* black tiger like that. No way. A monster's defensive capabilities were different when they were alive. The skins of living monsters were fortified by their mana gems, and they also used mana to make their claws and fangs sharper, harder, and more powerful.

Fina skillfully butchered the black tiger. Her technique was top-notch. I couldn't do what she did, with or without a mithril knife. "Great butchering as usual, Fina."

"Mmhm! Just like dad taught me."

"And the knife?"

"It's amazing. It slices right into where I need it to. I don't need to cut too hard. It just slips right in. Yuna, are you sure I can just have this?"

"Yeah. I mean, you're always helping me out. Consider it an extension of my feelings."

"Uhh, but...you're the one who's always helping me. You're always saving me."

Nah. When I'd just arrived in this world and couldn't tell my left from my right, I'd met Fina. If I hadn't met her, I wouldn't have any idea what to do.

I plopped my bear puppet on Fina's head.

"Yuna?"

"Thank you."

"Huh?" Fina cocked her head to the side, puzzled. I just stepped aside to let her work.

Fina gave it her all, as little as she was, and pushed on with the butchering. She stretched out her short arms, and when she still couldn't reach the spots she needed to, stood on her toes and leaned her short little body over the beast.

"Whew," she breathed out.

"You can take a break if you want."

"I'm okay. Oh...right," she said, and turned to me. "I forgot—Yuna, do you have time this afternoon?"

"This afternoon? I don't have any plans, nah. Why?" No plans to stop by a shop, no plans to work. If I had any plans at all, they were nap plans with Kumayuru and Kumakyu.

"If you have time, I think my mom wants to see you."

"Tiermina?" Huh. But why?

"Um, I think it's about the cake we ate yesterday. And she said she wants to say thank you for the mithril knife."

"I get the mithril knife, but why the cake?" Agh, I'd given Fina an expensive gift without even consulting Tiermina. I figured she might give me a talking to about that, but the cake? What, did she want another slice?

Fina finished up the butchering, and I finally had my hands on the black tiger's pelt. I gave her the black tiger's meat as a gift. I'd heard it was pretty pricey, but then again, it wasn't like you just ran into a monster like a black tiger every day. Fina tried to tell me she couldn't take it, but I wouldn't take no for an answer.

Oh, maybe we could take it over to Anz's place and ask her to cook it up?

Now that she was done with butchering, Fina headed out to get Tiermina. They weren't coming till the afternoon, so I decided I'd have lunch while waiting. After a quick bite and a mini-snooze with Kumayuru and Kumakyu, Tiermina came by, flanked by Fina and Shuri. I beckoned them into the house.

"Yuna, first, I'd like to ask you about this knife that my daughter has," said Tiermina.

"The mithril knife?"

"No, the other knife. *Yes,* of course I mean the mithril knife. Do you know just how much these things cost?"

Oh, no. Now Tiermina was saying exactly the same thing Fina had. Even if I told her that I brought the mithril in myself so it didn't cost anything, she probably wouldn't have it.

"The price isn't what matters. The butchering I asked Fina to do required a mithril knife, so she needed it."

"What could you have possibly needed a mithril knife in order to butcher?"

"Uh. A...black tiger."

Tiermina's face froze. "A...black tiger?

"I just gave Fina some black tiger meat, so please make sure to eat it."

"Ahh...slaying ridiculous monsters, as usual, I see. Hearing about the tigerwolf and the black viper gave me quite the start. And now a black tiger? You could have gone to the Adventurer Guild instead of my daughter though."

"If I did that, then people would know I fought a black tiger."

She sighed again.

"And—*and* Fina is my exclusive butcher. So it's basically my job to get her a knife she can use for butchering." Gentz *had* asked me to give Fina butchering work, after all. Fina had agreed, and we hadn't broken off our exclusivity agreement. It was only logical that I'd ask Fina.

"Okay, yes, I understand why you gave Fina a mithril knife, but why did you make a knife for *Shuri*?"

"I haven't made one for her *yet*..." At this very moment, Gold was in the middle of making one for her, but he hadn't finished it. So it was fine, kind of. A little. And anyway, I was just *lending* the knife to Shuri. It wasn't like I'd *actually* given it to her.

I explained all this to Tiermina at length.

And it was *exhausting*.

"Also, one more thing. What was that confection from yesterday? It was delicious. Are you selling that at your shop too?"

Right when I thought I was done…another question. Blargh. "I baked that because I wanted to eat it."

"You just wanted to eat it? Where could you possibly have learned to make a food like that?"

(I couldn't just say "*in another universe*," even if it was true.)

"Aren't you going to sell it at the shop? I was convinced that's why you had us try it."

Apparently, Tiermina had assumed the strawberry shortcake was going to be a menu item. She'd apparently planned to talk with me about the ingredients, pricing, and other things.

"We can sell it," I said, "but then the issue is who'll bake them."

"Can't we ask Morin and the others to do it?"

"I feel like they have their hands a little full with the bread right now." The shop was always jam-packed. This was always the case for Morin's bread, but the *bear* bread was way more popular than I'd expected. Mil and the other kids were trying their hardest to help out, but they always seemed busy. Cakes would definitely be too much.

"Is it difficult to make?" Tiermina asked.

"Hmm. I think it depends on how used to making them you are, but it always takes some work." If we were going to sell it in the shop, we'd need to make a ton of them. A single cake obviously wouldn't cut it.

"Yes, but I think it would be such a waste not to sell it. Can't you think it over after having Morin and Karin try it?"

She kept insisting, so we decided to have Morin and Karin taste-test the cakes.

"Well, then," said Tiermina, "I'll let Morin know. What do you think about having the tasting during their next day off?"

I agreed. We decided to call the kids to the shop for it, too...which meant I'd have to bake a *lot* more cake.

After we finished talking, Shuri tugged on my bear clothes slightly.

"Yuna."

"What is it?"

"I want some."

"You mean cake?"

"Yeah."

I still had cake left over from the day before, so I

pulled it out and offered it to the three of them. "Go for it."

Shuri started to happily eat.

"If it's that easy to make, Yuna, why did you only give us two slices? Gentz was sulking."

"Gentz?" Oh. Oops. I'd completely forgotten about him. Guys ate cake too, right? For some reason, I just had trouble picturing it, so I'd forgotten to prep even one slice for him. "Fina, why didn't you say something?"

"Um," said Fina in a small voice. "I forgot too."

Oof. Forgotten by his own daughter. Rough stuff, Gentz.

"Well, I gave him half of mine," said Tiermina. "He seemed to have enjoyed it."

An old guy with a cake? What an image. But...why couldn't some old guy enjoy a cake, huh? I myself had suffered the slings and arrows and other projectiles of people judging me based on how I looked. People should be free to eat what they want and wear what they want.

That said...if guys like Gentz were going to be enjoying the cake, maybe I should make a manlier version. Something less sweet, maybe. If I did that, I guess I'd need guys other than Gentz to taste-test it. The only candidates I could think of were Cliff, the Adventurer

Guild master, Gil, and, hmm, Gold the dwarf? Oh, Blitz was around right now, too.

I guess I'd start with Cliff for now? If I left Noa out, she'd probably complain about it later.

"But it really is delicious. I thought the same thing yesterday. I could eat this forever."

"Uh-huh, it's yummy."

Great reviews from Tiermina and Shuri, too. And...

Wait. Tiermina...didn't propose selling it at the shop just so she could eat cake whenever she wanted, right?

167
The Bear Has a Cake-Tasting Party
Part One

IT WAS THE DAY of the tasting, and the Bear's Lounge was closed.

When I left home, someone was standing right in front of my face—just hanging out right there, this girl with a backpack looking up at the bear house. Where had I seen her before...?

"So you really *do* live here."

"Who are you?" It was on the tip of my tongue. Where had I met her?

"You haven't forgotten me, have you? I'm Nerin. We met in front of Auntie Morin's shop at the royal capital."

Aha! Yep, she was one of Morin's relatives. She'd finally made it to Crimonia. So many things had happened since then that I'd completely forgotten to tell Morin. "But why are you in front of my house, Nerin?"

"They were talking about a girl in bear clothes and I heard she was living around here. Then I found this bear house, so...I wanted to thank you for what you did back then. I'll make sure to work to pay you back."

Work? Was she planning to work at my shop?

"Did you just get here?" I asked, and she told me that she'd gotten to Crimonia yesterday. She'd spent the night at an inn, and she was planning on looking for Morin's shop after this. She'd just stopped by to see my house on the way.

"If you're headed to Morin's place right now, I can show you the way."

"Are you sure?"

"Yeah, I was just about to head over there."

"Thank you," she said, and we began our walk together. "Your name was Yuna, right? Do you always dress like that? You were wearing the same clothes when we met at the capital, if I remember..."

At least she was being straight with me. I guess the average person wouldn't want to touch on the subject. "As far as my clothes go...no comment."

Nerin went silent for a second after I replied, but then she immediately started up on the next topic of conversation. "Still, I'm surprised you'd already gotten to Crimonia. I even took a faster carriage so I would get here as quickly as I could."

"I didn't use a carriage."

"Oh! Do you ride a horse then, Yuna?"

"It's...similar." I rode bears as my mounts, but that time, I'd used the bear transport gate. If she was going to work at Morin's place, then she'd hear all about Kumayuru and Kumakyu eventually.

Before long, we caught sight of the shop.

"That's Morin's shop. The two of them live on the second floor."

"Huh? You mean this place? It's so big. And what are those bears?" Nerin stopped in her tracks to look.

Since the shop used to be an estate, it was on the bigger side. A large statue of a bear holding some bread stood out front, accompanied by a bear on the sign and a couple bears on the second floor, visible even from here.

"Let's head in," I said, and she hurried after me.

"P-please wait."

Once inside the shop, we were greeted by the kids on duty that day. "Good morning, Yuna."

"Morning. Are Morin and Karin in?"

"Yeah, they're here," they replied, and headed over to get them. Morin and Karin came by immediately.

"Yuna, morning."

"Karin? Morin? You have a visitor."

"A visitor?"

"Auntie Morin! Cousin Karin! It's been such a long time."

"Nerin?"

"Nerin..."

Morin and Karin looked totally floored.

"Auntie Morin, you have to tell me when you're moving! When I went to the capital, your shop was closed and I heard you'd been attacked by men. I was beside myself with worry. I have no idea what would've happened if I hadn't met Yuna at the capital." Nerin pouted and folded her arms.

"Nerin, I *did* tell my brother."

"You told Dad? But...no one ever told me."

"Then he must have forgotten. I wrote all about how my husband had passed away, that I was starting a new shop in Crimonia, and I even told him that he shouldn't worry in a letter."

Nerin groaned. "He forgot? He *forgot?* Ugh, unbelievable!"

From there, we explained how we'd met in the first place. Morin nodded thoughtfully. "You met at the capital then. Yuna. Thank you so much. I can pay you back for the carriage fee."

"Auntie Morin, I'll work off my debts. Let me work here at this shop."

"If you want to work here, you'll need to ask Yuna."

"I need to ask Yuna?" Nerin looked at me and cocked her head to the side.

"This *is* Yuna's shop," she said.

"Uh. On paper, I guess, but..."

"Yuna, this is my older brother's girl, Nerin. She's been saying for a while that she'd like to work at my shop. My husband promised her that if she still felt the same way once she turned fifteen, we'd let her. I'd like to employ her, if you're fine with it."

Since she was Morin's family, I didn't mind. Of course, I'd ask her to quit if issues did crop up.

"Fine by me. But if she skips work or picks on the kids, I'll ask her to leave even if she's your family. You okay with that?" It would be an issue if she couldn't do the work, lost her motivation, or picked on the kids. No way would I allow that.

"If she did anything like that, I'd kick her rear end right out of the shop myself. I'd never let her come near the place again."

"I'd never do anything like that!" Nerin yelled.

Soon enough, Morin was introducing Nerin to the kids.

"Um, I'm Nerin. I'm going to be working with you from now on. It's nice to meet you."

"Are you Karin's sister?"

"Oh, uh! Not quite, but you're not far off!"

The kids introduced themselves right back. Looked like they'd accepted her right away.

"Wow. The bears aren't just on the outside, huh? The shop is filled with bears too. Was this your idea, Yuna?"

My idea? No way. Not a chance! There was a god to blame for the way I dressed, and as for the shop, it had ended up looking this way because that was what everyone *else* wanted.

"So," she continued, wrongly, "I guess you also dress as a bear because you like it, Yuna. When I first saw you, I was amazed at how you didn't get embarrassed, even when you were in front of people. It was so cute!"

"Hahaha! If you think *my* bear clothes are cute, then you've *got* to wear the bear uniform, Nerin," I said with a smile. I was only half-joking.

"What's that about a bear uniform?" one of the kids asked.

It wasn't a work day, so the kids were in their normal clothes.

"Mil," I said, "can you change into your uniform real fast?"

"Mmhm!" She headed off to change into her bear jacket.

"Karin, what's this about a bear uniform?"

"Uh! I know nothing, okay?" Karin dashed away, not wanting to get dragged into the whole thing. After a while, Mil came back wearing the bear jacket.

"I-it really *is* a bear. That's adorable. You work while wearing these?" Did she look *happy*? Or was I just imagining things? Nerin gave Mil's bear jacket a closer look. "There's even ears and a tail! Okay, I got it. I'll wear that while I work."

"Uh." I had been joking, but she'd agreed to it like it was totally normal. Even Karin was flabbergasted.

"Oh, I remember you saying something about today not being a work day. Is something happening?" Nerin asked. Come to think of it, I'd never told her about it...

"We're having a tasting today for this, uh, confectionary I made. If you'd like, you can join in. Give me your thoughts."

"A confectionary? And one that you made? I love sweet stuff, I can't wait!" Just the word *confectionary* had Nerin practically jumping up and down.

"We're planning on having others come to the tasting, so we need to wait for a bit."

Tiermina, Fina, and Shuri would joining us too. We didn't have to wait long for them to show up...but there was a party crasher with them.

"Why's Milaine here?"

"Why am I here? Because Tiermina told me I'd be able to try out one of your new confectionaries, obviously."

Uh. How was I supposed to respond to that? "Milaine, what about your work?" Wasn't she and the rest of the Merchant Guild supposed to be super busy from that tunnel to Mileela opening?

"I am quite busy, as a matter of fact...thanks to a certain someone." She'd just outright said it...

"If you're so busy, maybe I should close up the opening."

"You're always so disagreeable, Yuna. You well know that would only cause more trouble."

So she'd come all the way here despite being busy. Milaine was a hard worker and a good person. My impression of her had always been positive, but she *was* also the type who brought trouble with her everywhere she went. She enjoyed sticking her nose into entertaining things...or entertaining to her, anyway. I'm sure anybody watching would have fun, but I wish she wouldn't pull me into it.

We introduced Nerin again and started the tasting. Morin and Karin brought over plates, forks, and drinks. The kids waited cheerfully happily. Milaine sat with Tiermina, Fina, and Shuri at their table.

I started cutting up the cake I pulled out of my bear storage, Morin and Karin put the slices on the plates, and the slices of cake lined the tables.

The kids immediately started asking questions. "Wow, Yuna, what's this?"

"That's a strawberry shortcake. It's kind of like a pancake with fruit in it, I guess?"

"Yuna, what's this white stuff?"

"That's the main part of the cake: the whipped cream. Put that together with strawberries or some other fruit, plus a sponge cake, and it's delicious. Anyway, try some."

When I said that, they all started to dig in.

"It's so soft."

"It's delicious."

"The strawberries are so tasty, but this cream sure is sweet and yummy too."

No one looked like they hated it.

"Yuna, wh-what is this food?" Milaine's fork trembled in her hand...but she didn't stop eating.

"Like I said, it's a strawberry shortcake. We can switch up the fruit inside of it to make different cakes based on the season. I like strawberries best, though." I wanted to buy a stockpile of strawberries so I could eat it at any time. Thank you, oh, revered bear storage.

"This thought crossed my mind when you made the pudding and the pizza, but I *do* think that you might be better off as a chef than an adventurer, Yuna."

No, I wasn't cut out for being a chef. I was lazy, got

bored easily, and was all about taking the easy way out—absolutely not the kind of person who could spend every day hard at work in the kitchen. "It's easier being an adventurer."

"You're just about the only person I know who would *ever* say dealing with monsters and dungeons and other adventurer things are easier, Yuna. Certainly, there's no adventurer who's this cute and odd and able to make things as delicious as pudding."

C'mon, that was just my cheater bear skills and cheater knowledge.

"That's right," Morin piped up. "Thanks to Yuna, we have a lot more types of bread. Yuna is amazing at coming up with ideas, isn't she?"

Even Morin had started praising me, but those weren't my ideas at all. I'd just taught her about the types of bread we'd had in my former world. I hadn't invented anything new...

"So, Yuna," said Milaine, "I heard from Tiermina that we would be selling this at the shop."

"I guess it depends on what Morin says. I'd like to sell it at the shop, but I don't want to take time away from them baking the bread."

Morin and Karin were the ones who did the baking, for the most part. The kids just helped out. I felt like it would be asking a lot to have them bake bread *and* cake before the shop opened.

Morin nodded. "I can't say how long it'd take to bake a cake like this without trying it out myself. I might be able to manage with Karin and the kids' help, but it would definitely add to our workload."

Right, thought so. If it was going to be a burden to them, I didn't need them to bake the cakes. It wasn't like I was in a hurry to get them made. If Morin or the kids collapsed from overwork, that'd be way too awful.

I was the one who'd told Morin all kinds of things about this bread I wanted to eat, about that thing I wanted to try. We'd turned those into menu items and the number of bread options they offered had increased, making them even busier.

As I stood there hemming and hawing, Nerin raised her hand.

KUMA
KUMA
KUMA
BEAR

168
The Bear Has a Cake-Tasting Party
Part Two

"**P**LEASE LET ME BAKE THE CAKE," Nerin blurted out, raising her hand.

"Nerin?"

"I've never had anything as delicious as this before. If Auntie Morin and Karin don't have enough time to bake it, then please let me do it." Nerin looked seriously at Morin and me.

"But didn't you come to Morin's place in order to learn how to bake bread?"

"I'd like to learn to bake bread too, but this cake is delicious. If Auntie Morin is too busy and Karin doesn't have the time, I can make it. I want to be useful at the shop. I know I just arrived today, so it's not like I'm one to say anything, but I was baking bread at home. If you teach me how to make it, I think that I'd be able to do it."

"Morin?" I gave Morin a look. She looked conflicted, but happy nonetheless.

"Karin and I are busy," she said, "so we won't be able to help you, you know."

"Yes, ma'am!" said Nerin.

"And you can't serve *anything* unappetizing."

"Yes, ma'am! I'll dedicate myself to learning."

Morin seemed happier as she turned to look at me. "Yuna, I'm asking you too. Please let Nerin bake your cake. If she can focus on that, Karin and I will be able to focus on the bread. And most importantly, it would be a waste not to sell something as delicious as this in the shop."

"I'll help out too."

"Me too."

The kids were raising their hands. Nerin looked at them in delight. It was fine with me. "In that case, I'm leaving the cake to you, Nerin."

"Really?! You mean it, Yuna? Thank you. I'm going to give it my all." Nerin happily hugged me.

Milaine nodded. "Just let me know if there's anything I can help out with when it comes to the Merchant Guild."

"I'll look into the cost of the ingredients so we can start selling them at any time," said Tiermina. "Let me know what ingredients we'll need later, okay?"

There was plenty of work to go around, so I took them up on those offers right away.

"But it is delicious. I feel like I could eat so much more!"

Here I was thinking I'd made tons of cake, but it was gone in a flash. I'd expected the kids to ask for seconds, but Milaine and Tiermina had too.

"Okay, okay. Just remember, if you eat too much, you'll get fat."

There was a sound like a crack forming in the universe. *Crick. Crack.* The sounds came from everywhere and nowhere. I traced the unearthly noise...and found a group of adult women who had frozen with their forks still in their hands. Nearby, kids still savored their slices of cake with angelic smiles on their faces. The two great extremes of the world...

"Yuna, this makes you fat?" Milaine asked.

"If you eat too much of it, sure. Kinda pudgy, like, around your waistline."

"You must be joking," she asked with a strained smile.

"Do you really think I'm joking?"

Milaine gulped.

I thought everybody knew that sweets could make you gain weight? "You'll be fine as long as you don't overeat."

"Of course."

Milaine skewered some cake with her fork and brought it up to her mouth.

"Which is probably less than your six slices, Milaine."

"*Yuuuna!*" Milaine's shout echoed through the store. C'mon, she *had* to know that.

"Ms. Yuna," said Karin, "three should be fine, right?"

"Sure, if it's not every day."

Karin looked relieved. I still kind of felt like three was too much, personally, but she'd be fine as long as she wasn't eating like that every day.

"Shuri, here, say *ah*." Tiermina was trying to shovel the leftover cake on her plate over to Shuri. Looked like the word *fat* was taboo to Tiermina too.

"You're not fat, Tiermina, so you're okay." She'd been bedridden just a couple months ago and hadn't been eating well, so she was actually too thin. Even though she'd started eating healthier meals recently, she still hadn't put on enough weight.

Tiemina shook her head. "Yuna, it's fine while you're young, but you can't let your guard down when you get my age. Pounds sneak up on you, dear."

She looked incredibly serious, but...it wasn't good for kids to gain too much weight either, right? Moderation was the key to everything.

Tiermina looked at the stomach of my onesie. "And

I'd be in trouble if I ended up with a stomach like yours, Yuna."

I wish she wouldn't imply that my stomach was sticking out. It wasn't. It just looked like it was because of the bear onesie. No, honestly.

Fina was trying to reassure her mother from the side, "You're okay since you're not fat, Mom."

"Thank you, Fina," she said, giving Fina a quick and happy hug. It was pretty charming, but...really? All this drama about cake?

Still, we ended the cake-tasting on a high note. Other than my comment about getting fat, it'd been uneventful. Maybe we really did need cakes that were less sweet...and had a lower calorie count.

Nerin was going to work at my shop. She'd be in charge of the cakes, and she'd live on the second floor of the shop.

"Can I really have such a large room? I wouldn't even mind sleeping in the attic."

The rooms were pretty large, even for a former mansion. Morin and Karin were the only ones living on the second floor. We'd also moved the first-floor changing room to the upstairs...well, I call it a changing room, but the kids were really just changing into their bear jackets.

Although we had an attic, but we still had rooms available, so we weren't even using it for storage.

"Are you sure?" she asked again. "I haven't even started working here yet."

"Well, if you don't work hard, you won't get paid any wages." I'd left the wages and stuff up to Tiermina and Morin. Apparently, they'd decide after seeing her work ethic. Nerin had said that was fine with her, as long as she had food and a place to sleep. My job was to teach Nerin how to bake those cakes ASAP.

We started up cake-making practice right away that afternoon. We took the cakes we'd made to the orphanage. There were thirty people living there, so we wouldn't waste any of the cakes.

Considering she'd come to Morin in order to become a bread artisan, Nerin was pretty good at baking cakes. "Oh, I've always liked making treats!"

That was a pretty girly hobby. Unlike your ex-gamer narrator, I guess she was one of the popular girls...and here I was teaching her to bake a cake.

Still, Morin and Karin outdid the both of us. Morin wasn't just a master at baking bread; she was great with cakes too. She made it seem easy, like the artisan she was. Every motion was quick and efficient. I thought getting the whipped cream on cleanly was difficult, but she picked up on the tricks after making just a couple cakes. Soon enough, we could serve her cakes up in the shop with no problem. Her cakes were already prettier and tastier than mine. Karin was doing a great job with the cakes too.

It was so weird to think that Morin's husband had been even better at baking bread than her. I wish I'd had a chance to meet him.

Nerin had more than enough talent herself for sure, but she was a few steps behind the other two.

"Why are you making the cakes with me, Auntie Morin and Karin? Please don't steal my work."

"They're a bit like pancakes, so we could apply some of this to our breads. It's a good way to think up new varieties."

"Uhh. Then Karin, what about you?"

"I'm studying, of course."

Morin nodded. "Now, remember: if you aren't a good student of the bakery like Karin is, I can't leave you in charge of the cakes."

Nerin groaned.

"I don't want to hear it. You're the one who said you wanted to do this. If you don't do it right, why, I'll send you straight back to your father."

Nerin silently went back to baking her cakes.

Next to them, the kids were whisking away with egg beaters, busy making the pudding we'd be selling tomorrow.

"What's that you've all got there?" Nerin asked.

"Oh! Yuna made them for us. It's a tool to stir up the eggs!"

Since whipping the eggs every single day was a pain, I'd asked Gold to make them for the kids. There was a mana gem embedded into the handle that made the whisk on the end turn when they held onto it. It made whisking eggs, among other things, much easier.

"Yuna made that for you? Could you let me see that for a bit?" Nerin borrowed a whisk from a kid and started stirring at the eggs. "Whoa, this is so much easier!" She was really getting into it, like a kid who found her new favorite toy.

"Wow. Yuna, I'd like to use one of these too!"

"You can, but just make sure you get the cakes made."

And so began Nerin's crash course in cake-making. During the mornings, she'd help out with baking and serving customers. Once she had time in the afternoon, she'd practice baking cakes. Fortunately, she was improving steadily. It wouldn't be long before we could sell her cakes at the shop. She could be a pretty serious worker.

She wore the bear jacket the kids did. When Milaine found out, she had a jacket made specially for Nerin too. Apparently, wearing the same outfit as them had also made her a hit with the kids.

"Aren't you going to wear one, Karin?"

"I'd be too embarrassed to," she replied.

Wait, it was embarrassing?! Looked like I needed to have an in-depth talk with Karin sometime.

KUMA
KUMA
KUMA
BEAR

169
The Bear Brings a Cake to Noa

NERIN AND I had practiced too much and ended up with leftovers. Since we couldn't feed the kids cake every day, I'd kept it preserved in the bear storage...and I figured that Noa could help me with that, so I went over to her place. She could help me get rid of my inventory by tasting it, and besides, if she only found out about the cake *after* we started selling it in the shop, she'd definitely throw a fit.

Back when we'd started selling bear bread at the shop, she'd scolded me about it. "Why didn't you tell me!" Well, I would've if *I* had known about it. Actually, I wish they would've told me too.

The maid, Lala, welcomed me when I got to their estate. "Miss Yuna, what has brought you here today?"

"I brought over a delicious snack. Is Noa in?" I asked. She was in her room, so Lala led me over.

"Madame Noire, Miss Yuna had brought you a delicious snack."

When we got into the room, Noa was sitting in a chair and reading a book. "Yuna?"

"I brought you a snack. Were you studying?"

"D-did you really?! I was just about to take a break, so...no!" Noa closed the book she'd been reading and cheerfully ran over.

Lala looked resigned.

"If you have some time, Lala, would you like to eat with us?" I had way too much in my inventory. The more I could get rid of, the better.

"Are you sure I can have some too?"

"Sure! We're planning to sell it in the shop, so I'd like to get your impression too."

"All right. Then I'll prepare some delicious tea and join you." Lala left to prep the tea.

"So Yuna, what kind of snack is this? Is it as delicious as pudding?" Noa's eyes glittered.

"I think it's more like a pancake. It's good, but not in the same way as pudding."

"I'm looking forward to it."

While we were waiting, Noa asked me to summon

Kumayuru and Kumakyu to play, and her wish was my command. She played with them happily.

"Kumayuru and Kumakyu are so cuuuute!"

While Noa played with my bears, Lala came back with the prepped tea. I started preparing too, pulling an entire strawberry shortcake from my bear storage, slicing it up, and plating it. Lala poured the tea next to me.

"Yuna, what is this?"

"Like I said, it's kind of like a pancake." I lined the table with three slices. Lala placed a cup of black tea beside each slice.

"There's even strawberries in between the pancakes," Noa marveled.

"It's called strawberry shortcake. It's great with other fruit too," I said. Then the two of them picked up their forks, cut a bite-sized piece of cake, and brought it to their mouths. The moment they ate the cake, their expressions changed.

"It's delicious!"

"It really is. It's so very soft, and deliciously sweet. Is it this white stuff that's sweet? The moment you take a bite, the sweetness spreads all through your mouth. It complements the tartness of the strawberries quite well."

Lala gave me a precise evaluation of the cake. Noa just relished every bite.

"Are you offering this snack in the shop, Yuna?"

"That's what we've planned. You should come by to eat some, if you'd like."

"Yes, I absolutely will!"

"*After* you finish your studies," said Lala.

"Ugh," Noa pouted at that but didn't stop eating the cake. "It certainly is delicious, but it's so sweet that you end up wanting something to drink."

She sipped at the black tea Lala had poured us. Milk or juice would have worked just as well, but the black tea went nicely with it.

"This tea is a fine choice," Lala mused as she sipped her own tea, "but this snack is so sweet that I'd like something a bit more bitter." Yeah, I agreed.

But Noa had already added a decent helping of sugar to her own tea. "Do you think so? I think a sweeter black tea is rather nice myself."

"Madame Noire, that is because you are still yet a child. Your tastes differ from an adult's."

"Ugh, they do *not*! I could drink bitter tea. I mean, if I felt like it."

Noa finished off her tea in one gulp and asked Lala to pour her another cup. Lala smiled as she poured a new cup.

Hmm. I'd been trying to figure out all kinds of things when it came to the cake, but I hadn't put any thought into what drinks to pair with it. Although milk or juice would work, black tea would suit adult tastes better. But we didn't have black tea on the menu at the shop. Our menu was all about bread, so the only drinks we served were milk and juice.

If we just had tea bags to serve it with like we did in my old world, that'd make things so much easier, but of course we didn't have anything like that.

"Lala, is this tea expensive?" I asked about the tea we were currently drinking. If it was already expensive, that'd make it difficult to serve at the shop.

"Yes, this is our finest black tea. It's among Master Cliff's favorites."

"You're kidding."

She'd served *me* tea as expensive as that?

"Maybe I am," Lala said with a mischievous smile. I really couldn't tell whether she was serious or not from the look on her face.

"Umm, so would I be able to afford this tea? I think I'd like to serve some at the shop, so it'd be nice if I could get some that isn't fancy."

"Inexpensive tea is of low quality and lacks flavor."

"Could I try it first? Just to make sure?" We weren't serving aristocrats at the shop, so we could compromise on that a little. You can't please everybody all the time.

"But Miss Yuna, do you know how to pour tea?"

I knew you couldn't just dump out some leaves and douse them with boiling water, but no more than that.

"You can't just pour in the leaves and hot water, right?"

"Miss Yuna, I won't hear such tea blasphemy! You cannot savor the flavor of the tea that easily. You must determine the quantity of leaves based on the number of people being served, and you must control the temperature of the water."

Lala started lecturing me about tea very seriously. Hmm, looked like you couldn't serve good tea without working for it. I guess that'd make it hard to serve tea at the shop, no matter what kind I bought.

"Miss Yuna, are you listening? Pouring tea takes a certain amount of art. Tea thoughtlessly made is fit to be poured in the weeds."

Wow, she was really serving the tea on tea. I looked at Noa—she looked totally unsurprised, just eating cake and drinking tea like it was normal.

After that business, as we ate the cake and chatted, Cliff came by Noa's room.

"Father?"

Lala immediately stood up and bowed her head when she saw Cliff.

I spoke up at once. "I asked Lala to join our tasting, so don't be mad at her."

"*I* wouldn't get mad over something as trifling as that, though I'm not sure I can say the same for our butler, Rondo. Now...what are you eating?" He looked curiously at the cake.

"It's a treat we're planning on selling at the shop," I said.

"Is it good?"

"It was very sweet and good!" Noa piped up.

"Yes, m'lord. It can't compare to the pudding from earlier, but it was delicious."

"If you're fine with sweets," I said, "would you like some?"

Cliff stared at the leftover cake. "Yes, I suppose I shall."

Lala prepared tea for Cliff as he sat down.

She moved beautifully. Even to the eyes of a tea amateur like me, it didn't look like she wasted a single movement as she poured.

"It's delicious."

"Not too sweet? I was also thinking of making a slightly less sweet cake too."

"I suppose it is rather sweet, since you ask, but it's delicious nonetheless. But it does beg for some tea."

Cliff sipped the tea Lala had poured.

"I'd like to serve tea at the shop too, but it seems like a

lot of trouble to serve it. So...I have something I'd like to ask you for, Cliff."

"What's that?"

I looked at Lala. If I was going to serve tea at the shop, I wanted it to be good. "I'd like Lala to teach me how to make tea."

"You'd like *me* to do that?!"

"Even if I buy really good tea leaves, even little mistakes in how I brew it will upset the flavor, right? That's why I was hoping you'd teach me how to brew it properly, Lala."

"What do you think, Lala? The tea you serve is certainly delicious."

"Lord Cliff..." Lala seemed deeply moved.

"You may talk it over with Lala if you wish. If she has the time, I do not mind," Cliff said graciously.

"How about tomorrow then? I should have the tea and the things you need to serve it ready by then."

They also prepared some tea at a reasonable price that I could serve at the shop.

170
The Bear Is Taught How to Brew Tea

THE DAY AFTER the shortcake tasting at Noa's house, I returned with Nerin.

"Yuna," she said, "are we really going to learn how to prepare tea at the lord's manor?"

"Yep. I'm going to make sure you learn everything about prepping tea, Nerin."

"But to go to the lord's manor..." Nerin shuddered.

"No need to be worried. It's the maid, Lala, who's teaching us, not Cliff or something."

"That's still got me nervous!"

After thinking about where we'd learn to make tea, considering where the tools, tea, and instructor were, we'd decided against asking Lala to run all the way to the shop. We ended up going to the estate. It wasn't like I could let Nerin go to the lord's house alone, though, so I'd decided to go with her.

"Um, why am I here too?" Fina asked uncertainly.

"Because Nerin said she doesn't want to do it alone," I said. Fina was basically the only person for the job, considering her history of visiting the estate. "Plus, aren't you and Noa friends?"

"We're friendly, but...friends? Can I really say that?"

"I think you can. If you said you weren't, you'd definitely make Noa sad."

"Okay," said Fina with a happy nod. "Good."

Once we got to Cliff's estate, Lala was there to greet us.

"I've been waiting for you. I see you brought Fina too."

Fina bobbed her head. "Yes, thank you for having me today."

"This is one of Morin's relatives," I said. "She's going to make the cake at the shop."

"I-I'm Nerin. Thank you for having me today." Nerin bowed her own head like Fina.

"I am the maid, Lala, and it is my pleasure to work at this estate. It is I who is thankful to have you here." Lala bowed her head, and Nerin followed suit again. "I have finished the preparations. If you could come this way?"

She led us to the kitchen. "I have prepared three varieties of tea," she continued. "I believe that any of them would suit the cake Ms. Yuna has made, but each of them has subtle differences in how they must be prepared. Take care to remember them."

"Y-yes, ma'am."

Lala gave Nerin a gentle smile. "You do not need to be so nervous."

And like that, Lala started her tea-making workshop. She explained the varieties of tea, how much to use, the temperature at which to boil the water, and how long to steep each type of tea. Meanwhile, Nerin and Fina took frantic notes.

To serve as a model example, Lala had them immediately try the tea she had prepared.

"It's delicious," said Nerin.

It tasted great to me, too, considering I was more a tea lover than a coffee person. "It really is good."

"Um, I'd like some sugar, please," said Fina.

Lala chuckled. "Help yourself!" She brewed her another cup with extra sugar.

"It makes me want something sweet to eat," Fina said after trying it.

"Then would you like some of this?" I pulled the

shortcake out onto the table from my bear storage, and the three of us had the tea alongside the cake.

"Even less-expensive teas pair well enough with cake," said Nerin.

"Mmhm! It's real good."

It didn't seem like the quality of the tea would be an issue.

"Now, please prepare the teas for one person at a time, in the same way I did."

I thought Nerin would volunteer, but she shook her head. I ended up going first. Well...if I did learn, I'd be able to enjoy some great tea from the comfort of my own home, which couldn't hurt. So I did my best to brew the tea just like Lala had.

"Is this okay?" Once I was done, I picked up the teapot and poured tea carefully into a cup.

"Yes, excellent, Miss Yuna."

"Could you try it? As my teacher?" I placed the cup of tea in front of Lala.

"Ha! I warn you, I'm quite the harsh critic."

"You can take it a *little* easy on me..."

Lala chuckled at that, and took a slow, thoughtful sip. "Miss Yuna, is this your first time brewing tea? Simply put, it is *delicious*. I daresay I can give you a passing grade on your first pour."

Wow, that quickly? Well, she'd taught me how much tea to use and what temperature to brew it at, so it wasn't like there was much room for mistakes.

After that, Nerin and Fina took turns at brewing tea. Nerin's nerves got to her at first, and she messed up, but she nailed it on the second try.

"It seems you are all fast learners."

"We have a good teacher. It helps."

She'd covered everything for us in such detail that I felt confident we could brew great tea as long as we followed her instructions to the letter. I wonder how long it had taken Lala to figure out how to do this perfectly?

"I'd like to thank you in some way, Lala. Is there anything I can do for you? Give you all the cake you can eat or something?"

"That's quite the charming proposition, but all I ask is that you occasionally come to play with Madame Noire."

"Are you sure that's enough?"

"Yes. Not every day, of course, but it seems Madame Noire enjoys herself very much when you and Fina visit, Miss Yuna. Please do come by."

"I will."

"Me too," added Fina, "as long as Lady Noa doesn't mind me coming!"

Lala smiled. "Thank you very much."

Noa wandered into the kitchen while we were snacking down on the cakes and tea we'd made. "Oh, I knew it. Yuna and Fina are here...and you're all eating cake on top of that! Why didn't you call me? That's so unfair."

"You had your studies, Madame Noire."

"You didn't have to leave me out just because of that."

"It wasn't like we were trying to leave you out," I said. "And you know it. We came by to learn how to make tea today."

"Ugh, I do know, but...it's unfair seeing everyone enjoying themselves and eating cake."

"In that case, how about Fina and I brew you some tea?"

"As long as it isn't bitter..."

She wound up drinking our tea and liking it just fine. When Nerin had found out Noa was the daughter of the Lord, though, she just shook her head. "I could never brew tea for the lord's very own daughter."

Well, she'd have to get used to it. Noa was going to come by the shop sooner or later, so she'd eat the cake Nerin baked and drink the tea she made anyway. I guess I could keep her in the dark for now.

Other than Noa's intrusion, Lala's tea workshop ended without any major issues.

Now all we had to do was practice at home and at the shop. Since Lala had prepped the tea-making tools, we could practice at home...and I could also make great tea for myself whenever I wanted. The only issue was that it was a bit of a bother. Tea bags would be way more convenient, but that wasn't happening.

Thanks to Cliff's introduction and Milaine's work, we got the tea for our shop on the cheap. Really helps to know political big shots like the lord and the Merchant Guild master when you're in a pinch, it seems.

After consulting Milaine, Tiermina, and Morin on the details, we decided to sell the cakes by expanding the counter space where we stocked the bread.

Debut day for the cake finally came and the customers filed in, aiming to buy Morin's bread like usual. But with them came other customers who were there for the cake. Several days before, we'd asked the customers who were coming in for the bread to try bite-sized free samples. Okay, it was *partly* a way of getting rid of the practice cakes, but it paid off. Thanks to the free samples, the shortcakes were selling like hotcakes.

We'd set things up so that it'd be a little cheaper to order the tea with the cake than separately—a sort of combo.

The customers could still buy the milk or the juice too, of course. We'd also prepped some salted potato chips they could add as a side. A cake and chip combo—the most powerful of all combos, though just thinking about it made me feel heavier. Sure, it was great for business to let them eat cake, but maybe I could also make a poster warning people about the dangers of overeating?

Ehh, I'd save that until someone like Milaine came by and started eating six slices or more.

Tiermina calculated the price based on ingredients and cooking time. We'd priced it so that it was more than affordable for everyday people, but it still cost more than a piece of bread.

I mean, we had to make *some* kind of profit.

Cake selling was going well—we'd successfully sold out our whole stock. I decided not to mess with what was working; I wanted to see how things went over time first, then consult with Nerin, Morin, and Tiermina. Stuff like that.

"I'm beat." Nerin plunked down onto a seat.

"How was it, seeing the cake you made yourself selling?"

"Oh, it made me really happy. When I see people eating my cake with a smile, saying that they enjoy it, it makes me want to try some tomorrow."

"Looks like the tea is popular too," said Morin.

Tiermina nodded. "It kept us pretty busy, that tea. We'd have to prep it as orders came in."

That couldn't be helped—we couldn't leave tea to sit if we wanted it to be any good.

"It'll make things easier if you teach the kids how to make it next time."

"Nerin, I can learn!"

"Me too."

"Ohh, you're all such good kids." Nerin gave them a big bear hug. I agreed with her. They were all way too good.

"Nerin, everyone," Karin called out in the middle of the break, "we're going to prep for tomorrow in a few." The kids energetically answered, and before long, were on the move again.

"Sure is nice being young," said Nerin with a sigh. We watched the kids throw themselves into their work.

"You're fifteen, Nerin, aren't you?"

"Watching the kids just made me feel old."

"Then what, Nerin, does that make me a grandmother or something?"

"Auntie Morin?!"

Morin, who had been listening in on the conversation, was now staring at Nerin.

"Um, not at all! You're young, Auntie Morin! No one'd

think you were a granny." Nerin waved her hand frantically this way and that, denying it as loudly as she could.

"If I'm young," said Morin, "then you must be even younger, Nerin."

"That's..."

"And despite being so young, you're trying to make all the kids do all your work for you?"

"I'll—I'll start getting stuff ready for tomorrow right away!" Nerin got right back to work.

Morin watched with a smile. "She's far more diligent than she looks. Don't be too hard on her."

"As long as she gets along with the kids, it's all fine by me. And you're watching over her when it comes to that, aren't you?"

"I am. And I'll make sure to teach her well." With that, Morin got back to her own work.

171
The Bear Goes to Get Her Mithril Knife from the Capital

THE NEW SHORTCAKE was selling great, Nerin was working hard, and things were finally slowing down at the shop. I decided to head to the capital.

It was about time for me to pick up the mithril knife I'd ordered from Ghazal, after all. It'd been more than a couple of days since I'd made the order, and I'd already gotten Shuri's knife from Gold. It was safely in my bear house's storage, so she could use it whenever she wanted.

Since I was heading to the capital anyway, I decided I'd also bring some cake to Lady Flora. It'd be lonely going by myself, so I decided to invite Fina along. I was planning on a one-day trip this time, so I wouldn't need Tiermina's permission either.

However...Fina turned me down this time. I told her

I'd go on a different day if she had something she needed to do, but she'd told me that she didn't have anything planned.

Wow. It might've been the first time Fina had ever told me no about anything. What was this…this pain stabbing into my chest? It was like when you go up to your own dog, and it just runs away from you. I was practically close to tears.

"Yuna?"

"Did I do something to make you hate me, Fina?"

"N-no, you didn't. I don't hate you at all, Yuna."

"Then why did you say no?" She said she didn't hate me, but she'd always said yes as long as she didn't have something to do. Maybe she'd finally grown too old to hang out with a girl in a goofy bear outfit…

"Yuna, it's not that. Please calm down."

Fina filled me in on why she didn't want to come with me this time: she didn't mind going to the capital, but she didn't want to go near the castle for a while because of what had happened last time.

"I don't think that king would care much. And if he *does*, I'll knock some sense into him." I started shadow-boxing with a couple quick bear punches. I'd give that king a bear punch here, and there, and right *there!*

"If you did that, you'd end up in jail."

"Not if I don't get caught I won't." I could shoot off some air shots at him from far away.

"Yuna!"

"I'm kidding."

If he actually did try anything on Fina, though, the joke was over...and so was the king, maybe.

And so, alas, I ended up going on a lonely journey through the bear transport gate and arrived at the capital. First, I headed to Ghazal's place. It was time I finally ot that knife or he'd end up mad at me.

When I came out of my bear house at the capital, I pulled my bear hood low over my face and headed over to Ghazal's forge at a quick trot.

Unlike when I was in Crimonia, I was showered by yet another abundance of stares and murmurs about the "bear." A certain amount of attention was always inevitable, considering how rare the sight of someone in a bear suit was, but more people around meant a *lot* more comments and stares. As I walked, I avoided the thoroughfares with lots of foot traffic.

"Excuse me!" I shouted when I got into the forge, which brought Ghazal out from the back.

"Finally decided to show up, have you?" he said when he saw my face.

"Sorry. I had a lot of stuff going on."

"I kid. You came all the way from Crimonia, didn't you? You've already paid your bill, so you were free to come when you pleased."

Based on the look on his face, Ghazal seemed convinced that I really had spent the last few days traveling the whole distance the normal way.

Instead of, say, baking cakes and taking siestas and goofing off with Kumayuru and Kumakyu. If I'd really put my mind to it, I could've come back here using the bear transport gate to get it at any time—here he was, acting like I'd rushed right back when I'd really been putting it off the whole time.

Not that I could actually tell Ghazal any of that.

"Though I do recommend that adventurers come as soon as possible—even a day sooner—to pick up their items," he added. "When push comes to shove, it can mean the difference between life and death."

He wasn't wrong. If I ever ran into an enemy with magic immunity, the only thing I'd be able to rely on was my weapons. A mithril knife might've made the difference between a win and a dead bear.

"Did you get both of them done?" I asked.

"Of course I have. How many days do you think it's been?" Ghazal handed me two bundles wrapped in cloth.

I pulled one of the cloths away to reveal a knife in a beautiful scabbard. The grip was black and ornate. I looked closely at it.

"Is that a bear?" A bear face had been carved into the handle like it was some coat of arms.

"Looks good, don't it?" Ghazal looked pleased with himself.

"Did you carve this in yourself?"

"I wasn't gonna, but you were taking your sweet time coming to get it. I got bored, started engraving, and wound up with this."

"Um, sorry." *Sorry I couldn't be bothered to even come here to pick it up*, I apologized internally.

"Try unsheathing it." I pulled the knife out like he told me. It was a beautiful blade. When I held it up, the polished blade reflected the light streaming in through the window. "How's the grip? That black one you got there right now is the right-handed one. Hold it using the black bear."

"The black one?"

"Yes. The other one has a white grip. That's for the white bear on your left hand. Color-coded knives for you. Convenient, eh?"

I pulled out the other knife that was still bundled in the cloth, revealing a gorgeous knife with a white grip.

There was a bear engraved into this one, too... "You didn't go out of your way to make separate right and left knives, did you?"

I'd never heard of games having different weapons made for a person's dominant hand. But then again, there were definitely left-handed kitchen knives and stuff. I'd heard blades could also have slightly different angles to their edges that you could hardly notice. That was probably the difference here.

"You *did* tell me you'd carry both of them in either hand when you fought. I made them easier to hold for the hand they're made for, but you could use them with either hand."

"Gotcha. Could I test-drive how the mithril knives cut then?"

"Aye, tell me if something seems off about them. I'll fix them up right away, if I can."

With that, I headed outside of the shop and pulled out an iron golem from my bear storage, Ghazal following close behind. Time to see how sharp these babies were. "So I just need to route some of my mana though them?"

"Aye, that will make the edge of the knives change. The sharpness of your blade will echo the strength of your own mana."

"So if the blade can't cut, it's my mana's fault?"

"You tryin' to imply the quality of the knives I've forged is lacking if they can't cut?"

What could I even say to that? I guess all I needed to focus on was whether the knives could cut through stuff. I'd save worrying about a problem till there *was* a problem.

I grabbed the knives in the mouths of my bear puppets. Let's see...what had it been like back in the game? I hadn't worked with daggers much, but I'd used them occasionally. Knives are light, so it's easy to move fast while handling them, but they didn't pack much punch. Still, you could also throw them, and you didn't have to pack tons of power into every swing. Like any weapon, it depended on who you were up against.

After I gripped the mithril knives, I used the fundamentals of magic to gather mana into my bear puppets. Then, at once, I came at the iron golem's right arm with a swing of my right knife, followed right up by my left. The golem's arm split in two without resistance and fell to the ground.

"Whoa! Ghazal, did you see that?! I sliced right through the arm. It was all *swoosh, clang!* This knife's amazing!" (I was a little worked up, okay?)

"It's not the knife that's amazing, Miss," he said, beaming. "Even a mithril knife can't cut through iron as easy as that."

"You sure it's not your knife, Ghazal?"

I backed away from the iron golem a little. Then I ran at it and gave it a couple slashes as I passed by it. The golem clattered to the ground in pieces. *Beware,* I thought, *the bear ninja!* Oh, could I pull off being a ninja while dressed like this? The bear gear was pretty conspicuous, what with it being a huge bear onesie, but...maybe?

"A fine attack, Miss. I couldn't even tell how many times you cut the thing."

Ghazal approached the sliced-up golem and inspected the sliced cross sections, then he approached me. "Show me your knives," he said. I handed them right over to him like he asked. He held them up to the sky. "Not a single nick even after cutting through iron. That's power. *Your* power. You got the muscles for sword fighting, and the mana flows through you well. This is exactly why Gold calls you an excellent adventurer. Can't judge a book by its cover—you're living proof of that."

He handed back my knives, which I put away in my bear storage. Now *this* was a good shopping trip.

If only I could've fought the iron golem with these knives. I wanted to see if I could slice things up with them in a real battle. An iron golem you used for slicing practice was entirely different from one hardened by mana using its mana gem, like all monsters were. Too bad I didn't have anything to practice on with my new weapons...

"Still seems like a waste," Ghazal said as he looked at the collapsed iron golem. "If you're going to cut up iron, you could've used an iron rod instead."

I'd just felt the itch to try out my knives on the iron golem, though. "Speaking of which, I see that you've got that iron golem on display now."

"The customers like it more than I'd expected. They've never seen an iron golem in such good condition. It's a bit of a local novelty right now. Doesn't boost sales, but it's good advertisement."

I'd told him he could turn the thing into scrap if it was in the way, but I can't pretend it wasn't nice seeing it still there. After that, I took the leftover mithril from him.

"Well, thanks."

"Wait. Are you leaving those scraps outside the shop like that?"

Ghazal pointed at the scrapped golem. I hadn't wanted to bother putting it away in my bear storage. But when I started to clean up the golem bits, I came up with a great idea.

"Umm, it'd be a lot of work cleaning this up...so you can have it."

"Child, that is the stupidest thing I have ever heard in my entire life. Even chopped up like that, it's still good iron you're leaving me with. Do you even know how many weapons and tools someone could make out of this?"

"You say that, but I'd never used chopped-up pieces of iron like this."

"You could sell it. It'll fetch a great price."

I looked at the metal scraps. I'd chopped them up too fine. It'd be so annoying, putting those into my bear storage or pulling them out. "Nah, I don't need it. It's too much of a bother."

"Fine, fine, I'll buy it off of you. But I won't be able to give you much."

"Oh! What if we say it's a gift for you engraving those bears into my knives?"

"That won't do, Miss. I've already gotten too much from you, and I'd like to be on equal terms with you."

Dang. Now I *had* to take his money.

"And here's the letter of introduction to that master I promised you. I also drew a map for you. As long as you follow that, you shouldn't lose your way."

"Thank you. I'll go there next time."

"Mm. Please give my regards to him."

Finally, I thanked Ghazal and left the shop.

172

The Bear Heads to Princess Flora

AFTER I'D GOTTEN MY mithril knives from Ghazal, I headed to the castle.

They didn't look at my guild card or recognize my face either—they just waved me right in based on my bear-ishness. Right as I was going in, another gate guard took off running. As usual.

Looked like there wasn't much point to them stamping my guild card with this castle entry permit seal. You couldn't even see the entry permit without routing mana into the card. I guess the only times I'd ever use it was if I came across a guard who didn't know me or if I ever came without the onesie on...and taking off the onesie would come with way too many problems of its own.

I was strutting around the castle in my bear onesie. In any normal circumstances, a person in a bear onesie walking around the castle should have set the alarms off. Can you imagine somebody in Japan strutting around the Imperial Palace in that getup? But the people I passed by didn't so much as shout...until a woman popped out right in front of me.

I bobbed my head down lightly and attempted to pass by her, but when she noticed me, she started heading toward me.

What the—? I wasn't trespassing—I had permission to be here.

"Um. Bear girl, thank you very much for the picture book. My kids enjoy reading it with me." With that, she bowed her head and left. So this was about the picture book? I'd forgotten all about it, but I guess they had been distributing it to people in the castle.

But had word gotten out that I was the author?

Hmm. I knew I'd told Ellelaura to keep that to herself. Guess I'd have to bring my complaints to her.

It happened again before I got to Lady Flora's room. This time, the person even asked me for a handshake. "My kid and I are looking forward to your next book."

Was that my new job? Was I a picture book author now? No way, me? An author? I wasn't planning on drawing more—there wasn't going to *be* a next book.

I had to tell Ellelaura not to let this stuff spread any

further, but how'd they figure out I was the author when there wasn't even an author's name on the book?

Lost in thought, I finally made it to Lady Flora's room. After I knocked, I heard Ange's voice from beyond and opened the door.

"Oh, Madame Yuna, welcome." Ange was Princess Flora's caretaker. She'd even been Lady Flora's wet nurse and basically treated the princess like her own daughter.

"Hello, Ange. Is Lady Flora in?"

"Why, yes, she—!"

I was juuuust about to walk further into the room and say hi to Lady Flora when the princess herself popped her face out from behind Ange. "*Bear!*"

Lady Flora was all smiles when she saw me. She latched onto my belly.

"Hello, Lady Flora."

"Hello, bear!" She was so polite. Hard to believe that someone so cute could be a blood relative of the king. Yeah, she must have taken after her mom. She was definitely going to be as pretty as the queen in the future.

"Madame Yuna, please do come inside." I accepted Ange's invitation, but—right as I was about to go into the room—I stopped.

"Madame Yuna?"

"Bear?" Lady Flora asked.

"Well...Lady Flora, it's actually a nice day out. Do you want to go to the garden instead?"

See, if I stuck around here, the king would definitely come by. So I'd come up with a plan to avoid him. I'd come by Lady Flora's room more than once before, and I'd eaten with her every time, so the king would probably assume we'd do the same this time too. The plan was simple: I just had to switch up locations when we ate. Plus, the king and Ellelaura had given Fina a hard time. I had to get back at them a little, you know?

"Why, yes. Lady Flora, the weather is indeed lovely today. Shall we go to the garden?"

"If the bear wants to, yeah!"

Ange agreed without a trace of suspicion about my ulterior motives. Even Lady Flora agreed to my sneaky plan with a smile. Seeing their smiles kind of made me feel a little guilty, but hey, they were on board. My "The King Goes to Lady Flora's Room But Nobody Is There" plan was a go.

I imagined the king and Ellelaura's dismay at finding nobody in Lady Flora's room.

"Madame Yuna, is something the matter?" Ange asked. I guessed she'd noticed I was acting different. Apparently, I'd let my glee make it to my face.

"It's nothing."

"Is it? Well, Madame Yuna, I shall prepare the tea. May I ask you to watch over Lady Flora?"

I agreed. Ange nodded her head slightly and went to brew tea.

"Lady Flora, shall we go to the garden?" I offered my bear puppet to Lady Flora, which she grabbed hold of with her itty-bitty hand. Hand-in-hand now, we headed to the gardens.

As much as I would have liked to get there without anyone noticing, we passed at least three people on the way. I prayed they wouldn't tell the king where we'd been headed.

When we got there, we were greeted by the sight of beautiful multicolored flowers in bloom. This place sure did scream "royal garden." I'd seen it before, but its beauty really made an impression this time too. It was a great place to share a meal, though the denizens of the castle were the only people with access to it. Ah, well. I guess I could just be grateful that I got to share it with someone else today. And hey, if this place *had* been overflowing with tourists, we wouldn't have been able to relax and take in the flowers.

Lady Flora was having the time of her life checking out the flowers. Princesses and flowers were a great match, but a bear onesie and flowers not so much. Even imagining it made me laugh.

I took Lady Flora's hand and headed to the center of the garden, where a table and some chairs waited for us. The place had been set up for having conversations and dining. There was even a roof over the table in case it rained, and everything was arranged to let us enjoy the flowers. It was even protected from the sunlight with the roof, so it made for a great spot to eat cake.

Or so I'd hoped, but somebody had beaten us to the spot.

"Oh, Yuna and Flora. What are you doing here?" The queen sat alone, looking out at the garden. Was she really supposed to be on her own? Then again, this *was* the castle grounds, so it was probably safe.

"I was thinking of eating here rather than in Lady Flora's room today," I said. "Would we be in the way?"

"Of course not. May I join you?"

It wasn't like I could say no. But was I really allowed to give food directly to the queen? I guess it was way too late to ask that, considering I'd fed Lady Flora tons of stuff, but still.

"What are we eating today, bear?" Lady Flora asked, taking a seat to the queen's right. She completely associated my visits with food now. Made sense, I guess. I *did* bring food every time I visited. It was kind of like feeding a fuzzy little chick.

"It's sweet and very good. But please wait a moment, okay?"

There were four seats around the round table. Before I brought out the cake, I took steps to make sure no one could take the last seat, summoning Kumayuru and having it sit down next to Lady Flora in cub form. Then I had a cubified Kumakyu sit in the next chair over.

Now the king would have nowhere to sit even if he did come by. All I had to do was sit down and pull Kumakyu into my lap.

It was the perfect plan...or so I thought. But my schemes were ruined in an instant.

"It's! A wittle! *Beaaar!*"

Lady Flora leaped off of her chair and hugged Kumayuru in the seat over, before pulling Kumayuru off the seat seconds later. This hadn't factored into my plans.

"Oh, how adorable!" Now the queen was standing up and hugging Kumakyu.

Obviously, I couldn't tell Lady Flora or the queen to stop doing that. So we wound up with empty seats again.

"Bear, is this the big bear's baby?"

I guess this was the first time Lady Flora was seeing my bears in their small form, now that I thought it over?

"Nope. Same bears, just tinier."

"Wowwww..." Lady Flora squeezed Kumayuru. It was starting to feel like cake wasn't going to be happening. But she looked like she was having fun, so I guess it was fine?

Lady Flora ran around in the garden with Kumayuru. I was kind of scared she'd fall. As for the queen, she just watched while hugging Kumakyu.

"It's so fluffy and nice to the touch," she said. Kumakyu looked mighty comfortable in the Queen's arms. Meanwhile, I had nothing to hold, which made me feel kind of abandoned. "Your summons are cute, Yuna. I'd like some myself."

"I'm not giving them up."

"Oh, that's unfortunate." The queen squeezed Kumakyu even closer. That was beginning to look a little uncomfortable for Kumakyu...I wish she'd stop.

We watched Lady Flora playing around with Kumayuru. After a while, Ange showed up with tea...and with two *intruders*.

"Ah, we're eating out here today?"

"Yuna, what do you have for us?"

It was them. The king and Ellelaura. The usual suspects, all together. The last shreds of the "King Goes to Lady Flora's Room But Nobody Is There" plan dissolved into nothingness...

"Why are you here?" I basically knew, but I had to ask.

"Why, I'd received word *you* were here, so I left my work behind and went to Flora's room. Wouldn't you know it, though? I bumped into Ange. She told me that you were eating here today."

Where to even *start* with that? The king of the entire country left his work behind for *this?*

"Yuna, what is that bear playing with my daughter?" the king asked as he watched Lady Flora run around with the cubified Kumayuru.

"That's my summon, Kumayuru. I think I showed my summons to you before."

"That's Kumayuru? But they're different sizes."

Ellelaura laughed. "Oh, Yuna can shrink her bears." I'd told Ellelaura about it back when I was doing guard duty for those students, after all.

"Come here, Kumayuru," I called. Kumayuru came running over, and Lady Flora scurried after.

"To think that bear could get so *tiny*." The king picked up Kumayuru from at my feet. "Oh, and it's soft."

"Daddy, no take!" Lady Flora grabbed the king's legs and protested.

No take? How about these guys taking Kumayuru from *me?* My bears are family!

"All right, it's heavy, so be careful." The king handed

Kumayuru off to Lady Flora. Lady Flora was bigger than the bears, but she still couldn't carry Kumayuru and ended up falling onto her bum. She didn't seem to mind, though—she beamed and gave Kumayuru a big bear hug.

Bear...hug. When would they return my bear?

If I took Kumayuru back myself, I could see a crying Lady Flora in my future.

Uhh, what was I going to *do*?

KUMA
KUMA
KUMA
BEAR

173
The Bear Eats Cake with Royalty

IN THE END, the "King Goes to Lady Flora's Room But Nobody Is There" plan had completely imploded. Everyone had gathered anyway.

And—maybe Ange had done it when I wasn't looking—the seats had multiplied to five now. She'd moved *fast*. The queen was already sitting in a seat and holding Kumakyu. The king (who had abandoned his work!) and Ellelaura (who had abandoned...something, probably) were sitting down too.

"Lady Flora, could you also let go of Kumayuru? Maybe sit down with us?"

"Nuh-uh." The plan hadn't worked. Lady Flora squeezed Kumayuru again, and Kumayuru gave me a worried look. I was helpless to save my bear without Lady Flora crying her eyes out...

"Lady Flora, I have a yummy snack. Would you like to try it? You can't eat it while you're holding Kumayuru."

"Yummy?"

"Yep. And Kumayuru looks tired. It says it wants a break." I gave Kumayuru a meaningful look. Kumayuru *kwoomed* quietly like it was tired.

My bears were already accomplished actors. We'd tricked Noa with their acting in the past, and they'd played man-eating bears when I needed to threaten some villains back at an inn in Mileela. When Lady Flora saw Kumayuru acting tired, she agonized over it. But she still quietly let go of the bear.

"Sorry, Kumayuru. Let's pway again next time."

"Kwoom."

What a nice kid. Kumayuru crooned happily, and it wasn't an act this time. Lady Flora released it, and it headed over to me. I gave it a pat on the head as thanks for playing with Lady Flora, then dismissed it before Lady Flora could change her mind. She looked a little sad when she saw it disappear, but she still got into her chair.

Maybe I'd ask Sherry to make some Kumakyu and Kumayuru stuffed animals later. I'm sure those would make Lady Flora really happy.

Then I looked at my other summoned beast,

Kumakyu. Kumakyu was obediently letting the queen hug it. The queen didn't look like she was going to let go anytime soon. But her daughter had the sense to give up Kumayuru, so she would too. Or...or she'd better, anyway! She didn't respond to my silent appeals to her as she stroked Kumakyu on her lap. Lady Flora watched jealously.

At this rate, we'd end up playing Kumakyu hot potato. For now, I put my plan to rescue Kumakyu on the back burner and got the cake ready. I pulled a whole strawberry shortcake from my bear storage.

"It's stwawbewwy!"

Lady Flora's eyes moved from Kumakyu to the cake. Kumakyu wasn't in my hands yet, but at least they weren't going to be fighting over it the whole time.

"What is this thing?"

"It's kind of similar to the pancake you had earlier."

"Ah, yes, that the pancake! That was delicious."

I pulled several people's worth of plates and forks out of my bear storage and cut up the cake. When I started getting the cake ready, Ange started prepping the tea across from me.

"There are strawberries inside of it too," I said.

"What? I *love* stwawbewwies."

"It does look quite good..."

The cakes were passed around to everyone, and Ange finished pouring us tea...and milk for Lady Flora.

"It's okay if I eat it, bear?" Lady Flora held her fork at the ready, waiting patiently. Was it the king who taught her manners like this? Or maybe the queen? I thought it over for a sec and realized that, of course, it had to be Ange.

"Yeah," I said, "it's fine by me."

Once I said that, Lady Flora happily stabbed her fork into the cake. "Yumm!" Already her face was a bit of a strawberry shortcake mess. Everyone else dug right in then.

"It really is delicious, isn't it?"

"Yes, but it's a little too heavy on the sugar."

"You think so? I think it's just perfect."

I abstained from the cake and just drank Ange's tea. It was just as good as the tea I'd had at Cliff's. This was the tea of royals, so it had to be top-class. I'd only just realized it then, but all the drinks they'd prepped for me at the castle had probably been first-rate too. It'd be a waste not to savor them.

"Did you make this pastry, Yuna?" asked Ellelaura.

"Pretty much."

"I think this every time," said the king, digging into his cake, "but you're a bear of so many mysteries. You make these delicious treats, summon bears as beasts, even dress yourself as a bear, and yet you really don't seem like the sort of adventurer who can defeat such powerful monsters."

Probably because I'd come from another world by the actions of a god and had been handed ultra-powerful bear equipment and bear skills. Just *maybe* it was that.

"Oh, I know," said Ellelaura. "It seems that we're really in your debt for what you did at the mines. I'd like to thank you." How did she always know this stuff?

"It was a job." And she'd half-forced me to go.

"You still don't look like a powerful adventurer, after all this time. What do you think of having a bout against the knights and mages next time you're here?"

"Respectfully, I would have to turn the opportunity down."

Why would I want to do *that?* There weren't any benefits to me fighting in contests. If I didn't make sure I won the right way, there was a chance that knights or mages I'd crushed in the fight would resent me. There's nothing more terrifying that jealousy and resentment. I didn't need that in my life.

"I see. What a pity."

"Are you stwong, bear?" asked Lady Flora, face covered ridiculously in whipped cream.

"Your father is stronger than me, Lady Flora." Political power, wealth, and personal connections...those were kinds of strength too.

"Daddy, you're stwong!" cried Lady Flora. Ange wiped the cream from her cheek.

"Look here..." the king stammered, exasperated. I pretended not to see it, which brought out a laugh from everyone.

The cake seemed to be a hit, since Lady Flora's frown over losing Kumayuru had been turned upside down. Which brought me back to my next project: saving Kumakyu. It was still being held hostage in the queen's lap. There had to be an opening. There just *had* to.

Kumakyu gave me a miserable look. C'mon, I couldn't let Kumakyu give up hope. I could do it. I *had* to!

"Yuna, aren't you having any?" the king asked after noticing that all I was drinking was tea.

"I've had plenty from taste-testing it." I was sick of short-cake. That's what happened when you ate something every day, even if it was good. As the Japanese saying goes, you'll get bored staring at a beautiful person after three days.

"Madame Yuna, may I have a moment?" Ange said to me as I sipped at my tea, watching for everyone else's reactions.

"What is it?"

"Do you happen to have some cake for the chef?"

"The chef? Do you mean Zelef?"

That was the name of the guy. He'd thanked me after I'd handed over my pudding recipe.

"I saw the chef when I was preparing the tea earlier. When I informed him that you'd come, he...well, he seemed to be looking forward to it?" I think she was feeling awkward about it. I'd given Zelef a ton of recipes over the ages, thinking that it'd make Lady Flora just as happy as the pudding had.

I prepped two more new plates and put slices of cake on them. "Give this one to Zelef. And please eat some later too, Ange."

Ange would eat when it was just us and Lady Flora, but she didn't really do that when the king was around. It was probably a social position thing.

"Are you sure?"

"Let me know what you think about it the next time I come by."

"Thank you."

She accepted it gratefully and placed the cake on a pushcart.

"Ange, we're fine here. Why don't you take that to Zelef?"

"Are you sure?"

"Yes, I know he's looking forward to the food Yuna brings. You can eat your own portion with him."

"Thank you. Then I will take it to him." Ange bobbed her head and left the garden.

"A nice treat for them. You know, he's just one of the people who looks forward to your food, Yuna."

"I guess. I always come by without notice, even though he prepares food every day, so I figure I'm a bother to him."

In the past, I'd offended Zelef—the famous chef for the royal family—by bringing food without asking him. He'd apparently stopped saying anything after he found out I was the one who'd made the pudding. Since then, I'd occasionally send Zelef food.

When I'd gone to the mines the last time I was here, Ellelaura and Fina had said they'd go to the castle. I'd even had them take the new breads we'd made to Zelef.

A little while after Ange had left the garden, the cake on Lady Flora's plate had disappeared. She was staring down the rest of the whole cake, so I put another slice on Lady Flora's empty plate.

"Thank you, bear."

"That's a reward for letting Kumayuru go earlier." Especially since a certain *someone nearby* still wasn't relinquishing Kumakyu.

Still, this was all right. Maybe I'd bake a different cake to bring to them next time. Maybe I'd be able to manage a fruit cake or a cheesecake.

"Yuna, can I have some too?" Ellelaura silently held out her plate. If she wanted to eat way too much cake, that was her own problem.

"Yuna, if you could get me one too," the king added.

"I'd like one as well," said the queen.

One by one, I served them their cake. Oh, no, was I the new maid now that Ange was gone?

Since everyone's cups were empty, I prepared the tea like Lala had taught me and refilled them. I would never have guessed it'd come in handy at a time like this.

The king turned to me after finishing his cup. "You can brew tea?"

"And skillfully, I'd add," said the queen.

"Cliff's maid taught me."

"You don't mean Lala, do you?"

"Yeah. When we decided to sell the cake at the shop, I wanted to serve tea with it. I asked her to teach me."

"What? You're serving *this* at your shop?"

"Why not? I have the ingredients, and anyone can make it once they know how. And, uh, I'll also be able to eat it if the shop is making it."

(I wouldn't have to bake anything myself!)

"Then we'll be able to eat this cake anytime we want by going to the shop? Ha! Maybe I'll head back home to Crimonia."

"You'll get fat if you eat it every day," I pointed out.

"That's fine, since I won't let her go back to Crimonia."

"Argh, why is everyone picking on me?"

While we were enjoying the cake, I heard the sound of heavy running footsteps coming from the back of the garden.

When I looked over, I saw Zelef the chef running over. He was an older, flabby sort, but you couldn't judge him by appearances. He was the castle chef, and so well-trusted that they put him in charge of the royal family's meals.

And he was running right at us, totally out of breath.

174
The Bear Opens Shop in the Capital

HE WAS A PRETTY SLOW RUNNER, but Chef Zelef was panting as he ran into the garden. Ange walked behind him. For whatever reason, they were moving at the same speed. I'd never seen that happen before. Couldn't he just walk then?

"What's wrong, Zelef?" the King asked him.

"My king, and my queen as well. You two are both here?"

"Well, yes," said the King. "I'm taking a breather from my work." He sure took a lot of breathers, huh. A *lot* of breathers.

I guess if you're a king, nobody can tell you off. A lot of kings have this prime minister-type person who stands to the king's side and scolds him, ending up with stomach aches from the stress, popping antacids, that sort of thing. The king *really* needed one of these guys here, huh.

"What happened, my good cook? I've never seen you run before."

"Run" was generous. He'd been going the same speed as Ange's leisurely stroll. Ange, meanwhile, had gone over to the queen and Lady Flora to take care of things there.

"I'm ashamed of this, ah, embarrassing display," the cook said between gasps. "I was just so intrigued by the cake I received from Master Yuna earlier that I began sprinting in a manner unbecoming for my age." He paused and scratched his head awkwardly.

Unbecoming for his age? But he looked like he was in his mid-thirties to me—not that I associated running with any particular age. Actually, it was my personal opinion that some exercise would do him good. Get that stomach of his into shape.

Zelef looked at me without an inkling that I'd been making fun of him in my head.

"Master Yuna, it has been far too long."

"Sorry, Zelef. I know I always come in and throw a wrench into things when you're getting the royal family's lunch ready."

"That indeed may have been my opinion when we met, but now I too am among those who look forward to your meals. As a chef, it thrills me to my bones to experience your meals, Master Yuna. You reveal an infinite number of gastronomical possibilities!"

Wow, uh. That seemed pretty dramatic, but I guess everything's a little dramatic when you're in another world.

"Master Yuna, if I may ask, what is the white substance that was overlaid atop the pancake?!" Zelef rushed right up in front of my face and started to grill me. My bear clothes were supposed to be heat-resistant, but the onesie was still starting to feel kind of stuffy. Yeesh, some personal space would be nice...

I scooched my chair back a little and answered. "It's whipped cream. You take this stuff called fresh cream and whip it till it gets bubbles. All I did was layer that under a pancake with some strawberries."

How many times had I repeated that now? Well, it was the best explanation I had, so it wasn't like I could give them a different answer.

"Fresh cream, you say? I had not a clue such a thing existed. *Mmhmm*!"

"I still have some. Would you like to try it?"

There wasn't any cake left on the table, but I had tons of whole cakes in bear storage.

"If you have more, I would gladly eat it. However, I came here for...an entirely different reason," he said awkwardly.

"What is it?"

"Um, would it be possible for you to teach me how to make one? Of course, I would never reveal the great secret. You must have ground yourself to the bone as a chef in order to uncover such a unique culinary masterpiece! As a chef, it pains me to ask for a recipe, and I realize that such a thing is not something you are wont to reveal to just anyone. However. However! However..."

Sure, I'd toiled a bit to make the cake, but I hadn't been the one to *invent* the recipe. All I'd done was remember how to make it. I'd known what to mix together, but not the ratios—that part gave me a little trouble.

The king butted in: "Zelef, I was certain you'd promised not to ask Yuna how to make anything."

"Ah, but as a chef, my very soul yearns to know how to create this cuisine. I cannot even *fathom* the manner in which it was produced!"

"Yuna already taught you how to make pudding and pizza."

Zelef's head drooped and his voice dwindled away. "That is true, but..."

Just as the king said, I'd already given Zelef several recipes. But Zelef ran a tight ship, so I hadn't heard about any of them leaking. I didn't see why I couldn't share a recipe or two, on a personal basis.

"It's not a big deal."

"Are you sure?!" Zelef practically jumped for joy.

"Yuna, are you really sure? Every time this happens, I can't help but worry. Aren't recipes precious to chefs, regardless of whether someone promises to be secretive about them?"

I suppose recipes really might be precious to chefs no matter what world you were in. Maybe some people valued them even more than their lives, probably even more if they were secret flavors passed over the generations.

But this particular recipe was all over cookbooks, on TV, on the internet—it was everywhere in my home world, and I couldn't pretend that I'd come up with it. Plus, I was no chef, and it wasn't like I was planning on making a living being one in this world. Recipes weren't really important to me.

The only thing I did worry about was whether teaching another person the recipe could hurt my shop in Crimonia. I didn't want that to happen; the people there worked their butts off, and I cared about them. But as long as anyone else using the recipe did so far from Crimonia, I didn't care. Nobody would travel all the way from Crimonia to the capital just for a meal...and I wasn't going to let anyone beat me when it came to flavor.

"Most chefs don't so easily reveal their precious recipes," said the king.

"Yeah, but it's not like I'm trying to make a living from this. New cuisines are made by recipes spreading and by chefs putting their own spin on them. Sure, keeping a recipe secret might be important to a chef, but I'm not one. Not really."

I mean, I wasn't trying to profit off my knowledge of my old world or anything, you know? As far as I was concerned, tasty cuisine was meant to be shared. Maybe someone would think up something new from the recipes I taught them. What kind of wild recipe might show up in ten years, in twenty?

Not that I'd just share my recipes with *anyone*. Good food doesn't go to nefarious characters or people just trying to make a quick buck. I was fine with telling Zelef because he'd keep his promises, and he'd use his own judgment to tell the people he trusted.

He must've been thinking the same thing. "It will throw me for a loop if another chef asks *me* about it, though."

"It's fine as long as it makes Lady Flora happy." Beside me, Lady Flora took another bite of her cake, all smiles. That was enough for me. "But it's pretty high in sugar content, so be careful not to make too much cake. I don't mind what happens to Ellelaura, but I'd hate to see Lady Flora gain too much weight."

"Yuna..." Ellelaura gave me a look, but I ignored her.

"Ah, of course!" said Zelef. "Looking after the royal family's health and making sure they get the proper nutrition is my job. I vow that I shall not overdo, even if Lady Flora begs me for another slice!"

"I won't!" Lady Flora said, pouting.

Agh! She was too adorable.

"In that case, Yuna, why don't you open up shop in the capital?" the king offered. "You have your pudding. You could easily become the number-one shop in the royal capital if you set your mind to it."

"But I'd need tons of eggs for pudding, and don't get me started on the cake. That'd make everything way pricier. I've only been managing because I've made things at home."

Cake would need eggs too. They did sell them here in the capital, but they were several times more expensive than the ones in Crimonia. If I made cake or pudding with those eggs, they'd be unaffordable to customers.

"If that's what you're worried about, it's no issue. There's a village nearby that breeds chickens. We can issue instructions for them to increase their bird supply and their number of eggs, though it'll take some time."

Apparently, they'd already been given funding to increase the size of their flock, which had progressively increased the amount of eggs available.

"Um, I..." Zelef coughed. He'd been listening in. "What would you think of selling it at the shop I am planning to establish in the capital?"

"Oh, that's a fine idea," said the king.

Ellelaura nodded. "You're right. That might be the best way to do it."

They went on to explain that they'd been planning to establish a shop to train the chefs working at the castle. They were hoping to sell pudding at that shop, with my permission.

"I think," said the king, "that we could sell this cake at the shop alongside the pudding. What do you say? If you were to set up your own shop, you wouldn't have the same protection as you might if it were under the royal family's management. We would manage the recipes carefully as well."

"Yes, Master Yuna! I shall hand-select chefs that I can trust," Zelef added. "And with your consent, I'd like to sell the shortcake at a restaurant too."

Now that we'd gotten this far into the topic, it wasn't like I could say no anymore. I wouldn't have to deal with eggs, and they'd even pick out chefs for me. If I didn't have to manage the shop either, there wasn't really a *reason* for me to say no.

Sure, why not?

175
The Bear Rescues Kumakyu

WE'D DECIDED to sell pudding and cake at the shop at the capital, so I was going to teach Zelef how to make the cake.

I'd handed off my pudding recipe to him, but he'd apparently messed up while making it a lot of times. It wasn't like my directions had pictures with them, like Japan's cookbooks, so some things hadn't been clear. This time, I was going to demonstrate the process right to his face.

"Okay, I'm going to start making it now. Are you ready?"

"Are you sure?"

Everyone had cleaned the cake from their plates. "It looks like everyone's finished eating, so I think we might as well."

More importantly, I wanted an excuse to leave so I could save Kumakyu from the queen's lap. The queen *still had* Kumakyu in her lap, after all this time, and she showed no sign of letting my bear go.

She was still elegantly sipping her tea with Kumakyu gripped in her hands. Kumakyu's eyes glistened with tears from atop of the queen's lap.

C'mon, little buddy. Just a little longer.

Operation Kumakyu Rescue...begin!

"Heyyyy, so! Queen, I'm going to show Zelef how to make the cake, so if you could let Kumakyu..."

"Oh, I was listening. It's all right. I'll carry your bear over." The queen stood, Kumakyu still in her arms.

'All right?' Um, how is this supposed to be all right? What did she think she was doing? She wasn't even coming with us...was she?

"Make sure you don't get in Yuna and Zelef's way too much," said the king.

"I wouldn't dream of it. I'll simply be a taste-tester for Zelef's cake."

She was planning on having *more* cake? And queens were a lot of things, but they were *not* taste-testers. That was, like, the opposite of their job. Tasters ate stuff *before* the royal family to make sure the food wasn't poisoned or something. Well, that was the image I had in my head for how royal families worked, anyway.

"I wanna test-taste too!" Lady Flora blurted.

What was with this royal family? Were they supposed to be doing stuff like this? Lady Flora had already eaten two whole slices. I doubted a little kid like her could fit in a third.

"Well, then," said the king, as he stood from his seat, "I will be returning to my work. Yuna, that was—as always—delicious."

And just like that, the king was out of here. I'd wanted him to tell the queen to give me back Kumakyu, but he was gone in a flash.

"And I," said Ellelaura, standing up too, "will get that shop set up."

Was she not going back to her regular job? Was *that* her job? She was full of mysteries.

"All right, Yuna. Let's go," said the queen, nudging me in the shoulder and knocking me out of my thoughts. All right, all right, but...couldn't the queen at least give Kumakyu back to me already?

Please?

But the queen didn't hear my pleas as she started walking, still holding Kumakyu. My bear gave me a sullen look, its face resting on the queen's shoulder. *Oh, Kumakyu,* I thought. *I'm sorry I can't save you...*

We piled into the kitchen and, almost immediately, Zelef shut the door and locked it.

Uhhhh?

"It's to prevent any information leaks," Zelef explained. "Whenever I make any of your recipes, Master Yuna, I make absolutely sure that no one can barge in."

Wow, he really *was* strict about it...or no, this was probably also a safety thing. They'd prepared this kitchen specifically so that no one can sneak poison into the royal family's food, right? If tons of people got in, they wouldn't be able to tell who'd poisoned the food. The chef was thinking about safety and keeping people out of the kitchen.

Probably.

I pulled the ingredients and tools we'd need from my bear storage and began to explain stuff, while Zelef took notes. He asked me questions occasionally, and I answered as I worked. I guess Lady Flora and the queen were pretty entertained just watching too, since they were staring at me the whole time.

"I see. Fascinating, Master Yuna. You're quite skilled at this!"

"You think so?"

"Indeed! It's amazing what you've done at such a tender age. Why, you're practically on equal footing with my own chefs."

Whoa. I mean, he was talking about castle chefs hired

to cook for the royal family and nobles themselves, so they had to be impressive. Probably as good as chefs at a super classy restaurant. That was high praise.

"Is bear really that amazing?" Lady Flora asked.

"Yes, very," said Zelef.

The queen smiled. "Yes, she is. She is amazing."

Lady Flora nodded at them, then at me. "Bear, you're amaziiiiing!"

"Please, I'm not at all."

Since I'd finished the whipped cream while the short-cake had been baking, I scooped up some of the cream and brought it to Lady Flora, who opened her little mouth wide and ate it.

"Yumm."

The shortcake was done, so I sandwiched some straw-berries between the layers and slathered on the whipped cream. Then I decorated it with some more strawberries, aaaaand...done!

"A lovely little cake."

"Looks yummy!"

"Master Yuna, thank you so very much. This has been a most useful lesson."

"No problem. Remember to substitute out the straw-berries with other fruits that are in season too."

"Yes, naturally. I will scour the land for the finest combinations of fruit and pastry known to man or animal!"

"Yes, yes. But since you've already made it, we might as well have a taste," the queen said, eyeing the cake.

I guess we had to eat it now that I'd made it. But could she really eat more? She'd *just* had cake. It'd been a while since they'd eaten in the garden, but had it been all *that* long? Still, Lady Flora looked like she was really looking forward to it.

"I shall prepare the tea," Ange proposed.

"In that case, Zelef, would you be kind enough to prepare plates and forks?" I asked him. Zelef got right on it.

The queen smiled. "My, to think a bear girl is giving the head chef instructions. If all those chefs who idolized Zelef could only see this now, why...they'd be so very shocked." I guess Zelef really was the head of all the chefs in the castle, even if he didn't act like it.

Zelef didn't seem to mind, still busy gathering plates and forks. I sliced up the cake and put it on the plates he brought out. I made sure the one on Lady Flora's plate was half the usual size—she was a kid, after all, and had to have room for a healthy dinner later.

"Please have some too, Ange," I said. "I'll slice up the rest of it, so go take it home for your kid."

"Are you sure?"

"Yeah, of course!" I was pretty sure she had a kid about Lady Flora's age.

"Thank you."

After the tea (or milk, in Lady Flora's case) was passed around to everyone, we started taste-testing the cake I'd made...and there was my chance!

It was time to save Kumakyu!

The kitchen only had a single chair. Lady Flora was using that chair to watch me make the cake, and now she was using it to *eat* the cake. The rest of us were all standing. Since this was a kitchen, there were tables, but they were made specifically for cooking.

When the queen ate her cake...she would have to let go of Kumakyu.

She set Kumakyu on the corner of the table to start eating. My bear looked at me. The queen was eating her cake. I nodded, and Kumakyu slowly started walking along the table. After a while, the queen seemed to notice, but Kumakyu was too far for her to reach.

All she could do was watch. "Yuna, watch out for Kumakyu," she said.

"It's all right. *I'll* hold Kumakyu, so you just...enjoy your cake, Your Majesty."

She watched Kumakyu as she ate, seeming disappointed. But there was no way I was handing my bear back, no matter how sad she looked.

Kumakyu, meanwhile, was thrilled to be in my arms. Mission accomplished.

We finished the taste-testing, I answered some questions for Zelef, and that was it for the day. The queen had been staring at Kumakyu the whole time. She really seemed to have taken a liking to my bear.

Yeah, they were pretty soft and cute. Maybe the queen needed a stuffed animal—for Kumakyu's safety.

After heading back to Crimonia via bear transport gate, I had dinner and turned in early.

Kumayuru had played with Lady Flora. Kumakyu had humored the queen. Maybe they'd have a better night's sleep inside my bear gloves, but they always seemed so happy to be summoned when I called them for bedtime cuddles.

When I summoned them onto the bed this time, they snuggled in with me. "Kumayuru, Kumakyu, thanks for everything you did today. Take it easy." When I got under the covers, they moved to either side of me and curled up into balls.

I silently wished them a good night and fell asleep.

I never thought that I'd regret agreeing to that shop. If only I'd visited it at least once and seen it, I never would've let them make that monstrosity...

EXTRA STORY
The Nerin Chronicles
Part One

MY NAME IS NERIN. I turned fifteen a few days ago. I made a pact with my Auntie Morin that I'd work at her place in the capital when I turned fifteen. When I found out that Uncle died, I was so sad, but...according to my dad, Auntie Morin was still running the bakery. A promise was a promise, so I'd come to the capital hoping to help out, even if only a little.

Except the bakery was closed. No matter how much I called inside, I didn't see any sign of anyone coming out. I asked people walking by what happened, I asked the neighbors, I asked everybody I could.

They said that some frightening men had barged into the bakery. They'd trashed the place and had been violent with Auntie Morin and Karin. On top of all that, a giant man as big as a bear had apparently led the men away!

Some people had seen Auntie Morin and Karin after that, but they'd never reopened, and the two of them had disappeared.

Were they safe? Were they even alive? What happened to them?

I sat down and hugged my knees in front of the bakery. My vision seemed to darken. What could I do? Home was far away from the capital, so I couldn't contact my parents immediately...not that anyone was home. I'd lost my mom when I was young. There was Dad, but he worked all over the place as an architect in all kinds of different towns. I probably couldn't get a hold of him right away. I had no idea what to do anymore...

While I was hugging my knees in front of the shop, someone called out to me.

"What are you doing sitting in a place like this?"

I lifted my face and saw...an adorable girl in a bear outfit? She looked like she was about ten. That gave me a shock. I'd been to the capital many times before, but no one had ever dressed like that.

The bear girl started talking to me.

"If you're trying to get in, the bakery closed down."

I'd already found that out from the people nearby, and I already knew that Auntie Morin and Karin had gone missing.

"Where did you go, Auntie Morin? If you're safe, let me know…" They had to be alive right?

"Um, do you know Morin?"

Wait, did *she* know Auntie Morin?

When I asked her that, the girl told me that they'd gone to a town called Crimonia. On top of that, they'd opened up a shop there. It was such a relief to hear that! Auntie Morin and Karin were alive! I felt a weight lift from my shoulders.

But where was this Crimonia place? Even if I headed out there, I had no idea whether I'd have enough to pay the carriage fare.

I checked my purse. It didn't have much in it. I'd expected to lean on Auntie Morin a little, after all…

"I'll need to find work somewhere to save up…"

I'd need to find a cheap inn too. I'd finally been able to figure out where Auntie Morin had gone, but it didn't seem like I'd be able to join her for a while. Maybe it'd be best if I went home? No matter what I did, it was going to cost money.

"You can use this." There I was, agonizing over what to do, and the bear girl thrust her bear hand out at me…to give me enough money to get to Crimonia! It wasn't a small sum either. With that money, I'd be able to reunite with Auntie Morin.

But I couldn't just accept money from a complete stranger, could I?

"But, um, I—I can't accept money from a girl I never even met. I'm already in your debt for you telling me where Auntie Morin is. And you really can't just hand out money to people you don't know. Didn't your mom and dad ever teach you that?"

When I told her that, the girl in the bear outfit looked a little upset. Had I said something wrong? Still, she told me that she couldn't abandon me since she knew Auntie Morin. If I was worried about the money, she said, I could return it when I got to Crimonia—she lived there too.

After some thought, I decided to take the money. There wasn't any guarantee I'd be able to find work at the capital, so I'd work at Auntie Morin's in Crimonia and pay the girl back with that.

I asked where she was living, and she told me that I'd see it on the way to Auntie Morin's shop. (What was that supposed to mean?) Then she told me Auntie Morin worked at a shop called the Bear's Lounge. That seemed way cuter than something Auntie Morin would pick.

The girl told me not to forget the shop name, then left with the younger girl who was with her. I put the money away and headed out to the travel stop. I suppose it was time to get a shared carriage.

Shared carriages made stops in all sorts of towns and villages. The bigger the town, the more carriages you could find. On the other hand, if you were heading to a village, there might only be one carriage every few days or none at all.

When I got to the travel stop, I found tons of carriages lined up. Many of them would leave early in the morning. Most of the carriages there had arrived from other towns.

I headed into the building in front of the station and went to the counter.

"Excuse me. Are there carriages to Crimonia?"

"To Crimonia? Just a moment, please." He sounded bored, like he'd heard that a hundred times before. "We got some spots open on the following days for you..."

I chose the one leaving the soonest, then paid with the money the bear girl had lent me. Even after paying, I still had a lot left. I couldn't believe she'd hand so much to someone she'd never met. I definitely had to pay her back once I made it to Crimoni.

"All right, kid—don't be late now!"

I took the ticket, which had the carriage's departure time and date written on it. Now that I'd secured myself a carriage, I needed to find a cheap inn until it left. Sure, I had the money from the girl, but it wasn't as though I could stay at a fancy place. I found some budget lodgings and hunkered down until it was time to leave.

Nothing of note happened in the intervening time.

Several days later, I left the capital, headed for Crimonia. There were tons of people on the road with us, and we were traveling alongside another merchant's carriage. We had an adventurer as a guard, so that was reassuring.

As the carriage rocked me to and fro, I wondered why Auntie Morin would move to Crimonia and open a shop there. She'd been so excited to open the bakery in the capital with Uncle. I guess it was because of the commotion that people kept talking about. More and more questions accumulated in my head on the long, multiday journey to Crimonia, but I had nobody to aim them at.

Since we arrived late in the day, I decided to stay at an inn and then head to Auntie Morin's shop first thing in the morning.

"I'm pretty sure it's somewhere around here." When I'd asked where they had an inn at the station, they'd told me it was nearby. Finally, I managed to spot the inn's sign. This was the place.

"Excuse me." When I opened the door and went inside, a girl a little older than me spoke to me.

"Welcome, traveler."

"Is there room for me to stay here?"

"Are you alone?"

"Yes."

"Then it should be fine."

Thank goodness. The sun had almost set. Now I wouldn't have to search for an inn in an unfamiliar town.

"Would you like a meal?"

"Yes, please!" I was famished. I hadn't eaten anything but a light lunch.

"I'll bring you to your room first. Oh, and I'm Elena— the innkeeper's daughter. Please let me know if you need anything."

"I'm Nerin."

"Pleasure to meet you." Elena guided me to the room. That was super helpful, since I had luggage with me. "Did you come here alone, Nerin?"

"Uh-huh, I came here to see my aunt. She lives in this town." Maybe I could ask about her. "Elena, do you know where a bakery called the Bear's Lounge is? I heard it's in this town."

"The Bear's Lounge? I do, actually. It's a little famous around these parts."

"Do you really?! Do a mother and daughter work there? Named Morin and Karin?!"

"Ms. Morin and Ms. Karin? Yes, they do. Their bread is delicious."

They were here. Both of them were here! Thank goodness. Even when I stepped off the carriage and into Crimonia, I'd still had doubts that I'd see them again, but... it looked like I would! Elena told me she would draw a map to the shop later.

I left my luggage in the room, then headed to the dining room on the first floor.

Now that I knew that Auntie Morin was here in this town safe and sound, I could really enjoy my meal. I'd been almost too worried to eat for days. After the meal, Elena came over and put a piece of paper on the table.

"This is a map to the Bear's Lounge where Ms. Morin and Ms. Karin work." She'd drawn the map starting from the inn.

"Thank you. Oh, right. Do you happen to know whether there's a girl in a bear outfit in this town?"

The town was large, so there probably wasn't much point in asking, but I had to try. Even if a girl in a bear outfit stood out, that didn't mean that Elena automatically knew her. But she surprised me.

"You must mean Yuna. She wears an adorable black bear outfit."

"Oh! Yeah, that's her. Do you happen to know where she is? She helped me at the capital, so I'd like to thank her."

I told Elena the rest of the story from there.

"Wow," Elena exclaimed. "So Yuna dresses as a bear even in the capital? And she's saving people right and left, just like usual."

According to Elena, the girl was an adventurer who saved people and rescued whole villages. That bear girl was supposed to be an adventurer? Was she joking? Nothing I remembered of her matched my image of an adventurer. But adventurer or not, I still had to thank and repay her. She'd told me that I'd come across her house on the way to the shop, but I wanted to make sure.

"I think you'll figure it out when you go. Yuna's house is very obvious," Elena said, and smiled. She'd marked the map with a drawing of a bear.

"You might be in for a shock when you see her house," she added, implying...something. Anyway, I thanked her and took the map.

I guess finding out that the two of them were in this town had put my mind at ease; when I got back to my room, the trip from the capital caught up to me. I fell asleep the moment I hit the bed..

KUMA
KUMA
KUMA
BEAR

EXTRA STORY
The Nerin Chronicles
Part Two

I WAS FEELING WELL-RESTED when I woke up and got out of bed. It felt like the physical and mental fatigue of the last few days had disappeared. The weather looked great outside—it would've been so miserable if it'd rained or something on my first morning in Crimonia. I gathered my things and headed to the first floor with the map Elena had drawn for me.

"Thank you for looking after me, Elena."

"No need to thank me. You're going to work at the Bear's Lounge then?"

"If Auntie Morin allows me to." I'd made that promise with my aunt and uncle ages ago. Once I turned fifteen, they said they'd let me work at the shop...but there was a chance that the situation had changed. I still didn't know how things would work out.

"If you decide to stay, why don't you hit me up? I could show you around the town."

"Oh, I'd love that!" I said, smiling brightly. It seemed like I was about to make my first friend since getting to Crimonia.

With that, I headed out. Now...when I looked at the map that Elena had drawn, it said that the bear girl's house was close by, right? "Um, so Yuna's house is supposed to be that way, right?"

According to Elena, I'd know it as soon as I saw it. When I saw the strange building, I knew she was right. "Is that a bear?"

I could barely believe it. I tried getting closer to it, and...

"Yep, that's definitely a bear."

There it was right in front of my eyes—a house shaped like a bear. I couldn't decide if it was cute or strange. I just knew that it was...a bear. There wasn't any other way to describe it. Just like Elena had said, I recognized it as soon as I saw it. This had to be Yuna's house.

As I thought back on that mysterious girl I'd met at the capital, the door of the bear house opened. Yuna, still dressed as a bear, came out of it. She hadn't come out because she'd noticed me staring at her home, had she? No, she seemed surprised when she caught sight of me.

I still hadn't gotten the money to pay her back yet. For now, I'd just thank her for her help at the capital.

"Who are you?" Now *that* I hadn't expected. Yuna tilted her head to the side quizzically. I'd been so grateful to her, but she'd entirely forgotten who I was. I'd never been sadder in my life.

I explained to her that we'd met at the capital and, finally, she remembered me. Was I that forgettable? If I'd been dressed like the girl in front of me, there's no way anyone would forget me.

Yuna told me that she was heading to Auntie Morin's shop, so she'd show me the way.

But...how had Yuna gotten back here so quickly?

She dodged the question when I asked. Maybe she'd come by horse? I tried imagining it. A girl dressed as a bear on horseback—it was a completely incongruous image. There was no way anybody would travel dressed like that.

A huge building came into view. That was Auntie Morin's shop, apparently, but what was with the stone statue of a bear holding bread up front? I'd already heard about the shop from Elena, but seeing it was mystifying. There were bears on the signs, bears on the second floor... and while I marveled at them, Yuna walked ahead like it was nothing special. I followed after her in a hurry.

There were six kids inside, all between about eight and twelve years old. When Yuna came in, the kids were ecstatic to see her. Yuna talked to them for a minute, then they ran off further into the shop. Finally, Auntie Morin and Karin came out. They really were here! I'd already heard about it from Elena, but seeing the two of them doing well was such a relief.

Just...thank goodness!

"Auntie Morin, Karin, it's been such a long time."

"Nerin?"

I nodded. "Nerin."

They seemed so surprised. I explained what had happened until now. I told them just how much I'd been worried about them, and...then Auntie Morin told me that she'd already told my dad everything, from how her husband had died to how they were moving to Crimonia.

Ugh, so the whole thing had been caused by my dad being forgetful?! The next time I saw him, I'd have to really get on his case about it. Did he even know how worried I was?

Oh, well, I'd worry about that later. For now, I asked if they'd let me work at the shop.

"If you want to work here, you'll need to ask Yuna."

"Why would I ask Yuna?"

"It's Yuna's shop."

Now I had even more questions. What did she mean about this being *Yuna's* shop? I looked at Yuna for answers, but she just looked tired of talking about it.

I just had no idea what was going on anymore.

"Yuna, this is my older brother's girl, Nerin. She's been saying for a while that she'd like to work at my shop. My husband promised her that if she still felt the same way once she turned fifteen, we'd let her. I'd like to employ her, if you're fine with it."

Yuna said I could work, as long as I didn't skip out or pick on the kids. Not that I'd do either of those things! I was going to work my butt off, and I'd never bully kids.

I gave the children a smile and a greeting to show them I was friendly. They responded in kind. They were pretty cute! *Everything* was cute; both the shop and the kids. I was excited to start work.

The only thing I hadn't expected was that I'd be dressed as a bear while working. A girl named Mil showed me the bear uniform. Yuna's bear clothes were baggy, but Mil's bear outfit was designed to go right over her regular clothes. She even had a tail on her bum!

Apparently, the kids dressed as bears while they worked. I was told I'd have to dress the same way if I wanted the job.

I just blurted out that I'd do it. It was a little embarrassing when you thought about it. But if I refused, there was a chance I'd be out of a job. Plus, Mil looked so adorable dressed as a bear. Would I look that cute? Or...oh, it didn't matter. As long as I worked hard, almost any outfit would do.

They were going to taste-test some new confectionary, so they asked me to try it out too. Would it be good? I was starting to look forward to it.

Meanwhile, I looked around the store. It was filled to the brim with bears. There were bears on the walls and pillars too, each table with its own posed bear. The one at the table I was sitting at was doing a handstand!

They were all adorable. I guess that's just what Yuna liked. I'd never met someone so infatuated with bears... but I sort of wished she wouldn't drag me and my own fashion choices into it.

While I was looking around the shop, the door opened. Two adult ladies and two girls came in. I'd seen one of the girls before–she was definitely the one who'd accompanied Yuna at the capital.

The girl from the capital was named Fina, the other girl was her sister Shuri, and the nice-looking lady was Tiermina. Tiermina was their mother, and she did everything for the shop behind the scenes.

The serious-looking lady with her was the Merchant Guild's master, Milaine. I was so surprised that someone so powerful would be at a taste-testing. Anyone involved in business would be overly nice to the Merchant Guild master, but Yuna was pretty hard on Milaine. Just who *was* Yuna?

Once all of us were gathered, Yuna brought out a white, round confectionary with strawberries on top from...her bear glove?! Was that bear glove an item bag?

Yuna cut into the round thing with a knife and started serving it on plates for all of us, including me. When I looked closely at the thing, it looked like layers of soft bread. Sandwiched between the layers was white stuff and some strawberries. She called it "strawberry shortcake."

Once we each had a plate, we started the tasting.

The soft shortcake broke apart with my fork easily. I took a bite and the cake's sweetness filled my mouth.. The strawberries went splendidly with the white stuff! I scooped up some of that white stuff onto my fork and licked it. The moment it touched my tongue, it melted. The sweetness spread throughout my mouth.

I couldn't stop eating! All of us just kept saying just how delicious it was.

Had Yuna—this girl in a bear outfit—really made

something this delicious? I couldn't stop looking at her now. Really, just *who was Yuna*?

Elena from the inn had said that Yuna was an adventurer, but for a girl this cute, that just couldn't be...right? She had to be joking. Had she really been pulling a prank on me? Elena didn't *seem* like that type of person.

The mysteries surrounding Yuna just kept multiplying.

We kept going with the tasting, and they started talking about how the strawberry shortcake was going to be sold at the shop.

I agreed. They simply had to sell it! I'd never had a confectionary as delicious as this before. Maybe the upper-class families and aristocracy had eaten this before, but a commoner like me? Never! If it started selling here, normal people like me could have it too.

Auntie Morin and Yuna went back and forth about details, considering all kinds of things. Auntie Morin didn't know whether they had time to make it—or enough people. In the end, Auntie Morin and Karin concluded that there wasn't enough time to bake the cake every day.

But I couldn't allow it. I took a small, deep breath, then spoke up. "Please let me bake the cake."

After a lot more talk and way more details, it was decided that I'd be making the cakes.

I was thrilled by that, but...could I really do it? There was no going back after blurting that out, though. If Auntie Morin and Karin couldn't do it, then I'd have to take up the mantle of cake.

Later that evening on that day, Auntie Morin and Karin told me all about what had happened to them until now.

When Uncle had passed away, they'd fallen prey to a terrible merchant, been attacked by ruffians, and almost had their bakery taken from them. But Yuna had appeared and saved them. Then, she'd invited them to open up a bakery in Crimonia, gotten them a location—the building we all worked in—and all the things they'd needed for a shop. Just imagining how much all of that cost sent shivers down my spine.

"Is Yuna from a rich family?" I asked.

"Hmm. She claims herself that she's just an adventurer, but I don't know any other details. I'm not one to ask, and you shouldn't either. People have things they can't talk about, Nerin."

But I really, really wanted to ask her about it! The mysteries surrounding her just kept mounting...even if Elena and now Karin had both told me that Yuna was an adventurer.

"I know she doesn't look like one, but she really is a powerful adventurer," Karin had said. "She beat up these huge men when she saved us too."

Hmm. I doubted that both Elena and Karin would lie, but I just couldn't even imagine Yuna fighting.

"Yuna is incredibly kind," they told me. I already knew that. She'd talked to me in the capital when I was in trouble and had lent me so much money. The kids seemed to really adore her too.

"That's because she rescued them," they told me.

She'd saved all the kids at the orphanage. Tons of people would turn a blind eye to something like that. Some might offer a helping hand, but most wealthy people stopped short at offering money and food. Yuna, on the other hand, had given the kids work that let them survive by themselves. She hadn't forced them to work, either.

"She even gives them breaks. She's so kind, and she really does think of what's in the kids' best interests. She said she's having the kids work at the shop so that when they grow up, they'll have a job. I've even taught the kids how to bake bread. The thought of the recipe your Uncle and I thought up, along with some of Yuna's creations, spreading around just makes me so happy!"

Auntie Morin really did seem happy, yeah!

But...seriously, just *who was Yuna*? The mysteries were almost tripping over each other!

We practiced making the cake the next day. The kids would help Auntie Morin in the morning, and I'd help with the customers when the shop opened.

"We're fine here, Nerin, so you can go practice baking with Yuna," Karin said while I was cleaning shop. I accepted Karin's proposal and went to practice. Hopefully, I could get a little better or faster through repetition. Even if I made a spectacularly tasty cake, it wouldn't matter if I was too slow. Developing my technique and speed was just another reason to practice.

I knew that because I'd helped out at Auntie Morin's bakery in the capital. Trying to make anything would cost money because of ingredient and labor expenses. If I took hours making a single cake, she couldn't pay my wages.

Yuna told me to practice and that I could use tons of eggs. At first, I'd been nervous about using them, but then I found out that the kids went through a hundred eggs a day just for pudding. When I saw them doing that, I relaxed.

Whenever the kids had spare time, they'd make pudding. At first I was like...what *is* pudding? But then I found out it was this delicious treat. Amazingly enough, Yuna had made that too.

I was shocked when I saw the kids kneading the dough for bread and making pudding like they knew exactly what they were doing. I couldn't let a bunch of kids outdo me.

Wow. This shop was a strange place.

While I was practicing, Yuna suddenly told us that we'd serve tea at the shop too. I suppose tea would go well with cake, considering how sweet it was, but I couldn't have ever guessed that we'd go to the feudal lord's very own estate in order to learn how to serve it.

It was the most nerve-wracking experience in my entire life. I only learned later, but the lord was Yuna's acquaintance. He and his daughter would stop by the shop to buy bread and eat. *What was even going on with this place?* The feudal lord himself was visiting the shop? I'd never heard of such a thing. And Fina was friends with the lord's daughter?!

I couldn't wrap my mind around it anymore.

The day finally came, and it was time to put out the cakes I'd made in the shop. I was so nervous the night before, I could hardly sleep. What if they didn't sell?

What if people said they tasted terrible? So many things swirled in the back of my mind. I'd never thought I'd be so sensitive about this stuff. I pulled the covers over me and closed my eyes. I just wanted to sleep...

The sunlight streaming in from the window woke me up. I guess I had fallen asleep at some point.

I changed immediately and headed to the kitchen. I had my normal meal for breakfast, which was bread baked by Auntie Morin and Karin.

From there, I started making cakes with help from the kids. I made the shortcakes and spread whipped cream on them. Then I used this tool that squeezes out the whipped cream to make the decorations. This was the hardest part. If all of it wasn't even, it wouldn't look nice. Nervous as I was, I still decorated the cake with whipped cream.

"Whew!" Cleanly too, somehow. After that, I decorated the cake evenly with strawberries and cut it into slices. I needed to slice the cake evenly too, or we'd get customer complaints. With a few more clean cuts, the cake was done.

Now I just had to do it again.

The cakes I'd made lined the shelves in the shop.

I was nervous. What if no one bought any? What if *everyone* bought them and said they didn't taste good? I was a ball of nerves. I hadn't messed up somewhere, had I? I hadn't mixed up the salt for the sugar, had I?!

The door to the shop opened. Our normal customers came to buy bread as usual. And then there was someone who ordered the cake. It was an easygoing woman in her mid-twenties. She was my first customer.

She ordered the tea along with it, so I prepared that just like Lala had taught me. The customer took the cake and tea and went to sit down. I followed her with my eyes.

When she took a bite of the cake, her face broke out into a smile and she ate the whole thing up. I was so giddy! We kept selling cakes until we were sold out.

I'd been overflowing with emotions the whole day from anxiety, relief, excitement, happiness, joy, and gratitude.

I'd never forget that day...even if we were way, way too busy!

The Rookie Adventurers Mature

"**H**ORN, stop the wolf coming from the right. Brute and I will take the vanguard. Lahtte, use your bow if you get the chance."

I gave everyone directions while I attacked the wolf in front of me. When I kept all the stuff Ms. Yuna had taught me in mind, I started noticing all kinds of things.

While I practiced looking at the entire enemy, I started to notice things around me rather than just the enemy right in front of me. I started to notice how my teammates were fighting, whether they were in danger, and if they were freed up, which made giving directions easier.

The only issue was that I'd get distracted from what was going on around *me* and lose my concentration, which could put me in danger.

Ms. Yuna had told me that it's sometimes most

important to focus on the enemy at hand, and that I'd need to judge for myself when it was time to change focus. Ms. Yuna sure liked to make things complicated.

Still, we wouldn't get flustered anymore when multiple wolves or goblins showed up. Brandaugh had taught Lahtte about the bow, Brute had learned how to fight from Gil, and Horn's magic had gotten better thanks to Ms. Yuna. I'd gotten stronger too from Ms. Yuna and Gil teaching me.

Not that we hadn't learned from other adventurers too. I was definitely stronger compared to when I'd come to Crimonia. Since my parents were probably worried about me, it was probably time to visit the village.

When we came to give our report, Ms. Helen seemed pleased with us. "Your group really has gotten stronger, Shin. I was worried about you when you first got here, but you've really improved in these last few months."

It kind of felt like she was praising us. Brought my spirits up, you know?

"It's all because Ms. Yuna taught me how to use magic," Horn replied in my place. Horn really had gotten better at magic. Thanks to Ms. Yuna's instruction, her once-wimpy spells could take down a wolf single-handedly.

A while ago, Horn had even considered getting a bear outfit...but I don't think that would've helped quite so much.

"Ha! It seems you've taken quite the liking to Ms. Yuna, Horn, haven't you?"

Horn looked mighty pleased at that. She really did love Ms. Yuna. There weren't many people around who'd be so thorough about teaching somebody how to use magic. Plus, Ms. Yuna would treat Horn to lunch whenever they met up. It was kind of unfair that she was getting all the attention, but—according to Horn, at least—she couldn't stand it, since it felt like a younger girl was treating her to stuff. I couldn't tell how old Ms. Yuna was, but Horn seemed a little older. Didn't make a difference to me either way, but I think that bear outfit made Ms. Yuna seem younger to Horn.

"Ms. Helen, do you know exactly what Ms. Yuna is?" I asked. "Her magic's amazing, and she's great at sword-fighting too."

"Normally, I'd just tell you that I can't disclose personal information, but I don't have anything to disclose in the first place. I have no idea where she came from, why she's alone, or what possessed her to dress like a bear."

"I think," said Horn, "that she must have come from the country of the bears."

It sounded like poppycock to me, but Ms. Helen took it seriously. "That really might be the case. Her beast summons, Kumayuru and Kumakyu, are bears. She lives in a bear house too, after all."

Okay, okay, she had a point. But...a country of bears out there? No chance.

Anyway, we finished giving our report and got our reward. We'd be eating good tonight! When we tried to leave, though, Ms. Helen called out to stop us.

"Oh, right. Shin—all of you—I have a job available to patrol the woods. Would you like to take it?" Ms. Helen asked like she'd just remembered.

"Patrol how?"

"Check the area around the woods to make sure monsters don't make their way to the highways."

Right, I'd heard of jobs like that. Adventurers periodically went on patrol around the town and the highways to make sure that everything was safe. If a bunch of monsters appeared, the adventurers notified the guild. Then, depending on how many monsters there were, they'd determine what rank of adventurer they needed to deal with them. In other words, the job was just to check for monster appearances.

We could collect cash just by looking around, no monster-slaying necessary. Sure, it was easy to lose trust from fellow adventurers if you faked the report and got caught, but if you took it seriously? It was hard to find a better gig.

"I think you can handle it," said Ms. Helen, "considering how you're doing now."

It wasn't like the job didn't come with risks. But the fact that the guild was giving us this job meant that they really did recognize our skill. I looked at Horn and the rest of the gang. Horn and the others gave me a little nod.

"We'll do it," I said. "Absolutely."

"Excellent. This is the map of the woods. Please don't forget to bring back the details of where you went, where you saw the monsters, and what you killed."

When we told Ms. Yuna about the job, she seemed super shocked. She was all like "That's seriously a quest?!" Well, not for her—she was way too strong to do stuff like this.

We headed out into the woods to start exploring.

"We'll get a reward just for hanging out in the woods," I said with a smile. "What a piece of cake."

"But we still have to actually patrol them," Brute pointed out.

"You don't have to tell me that. Look, we're going to be visiting this place all the time. It'll be good to learn more about it."

If we got attacked by monsters sometime and had to scram, there was a chance we'd get lost in the woods. Learning more about the geography could help us know which way to escape.

The worst thing that could happen was if we were driven to a cliff. Getting a sense of our surroundings was going to be important.

"I don't see any monsters," said Lahtte.

"I wish at least a few would turn up." If we slayed any, we'd get an additional reward.

"Shin," Brute warned, "don't let your guard down."

"I know that. I'm counting on you to keep an eye out behind us, Brute."

I took the lead, followed by Horn and Lahtte in that order, with Brute at our rear. I regularly checked the map against our surroundings as we pressed forward. We crossed a stream at some point and came out to this panoramic view, exactly like the map told us we would.

"This would be an easy place to fight. Plenty of space."

"Yeah, we were taking a risk walking around the mountainous terrain earlier since we didn't have a way to escape." We'd just crossed over a tall, craggy mountain earlier, which wasn't really conducive to high-tailing it out of there.

"Shin, look over there. It's a goblin."

Three of them, actually, with their backs to us.

"Should we slay them?"

"Yeah. If they get to the highway, that'll be a hazard. Let's take 'em out."

If we didn't get them now, we'd leave any travelers in danger. No, we had to fight.

We got rid of those three goblins...and it was no problem. The problem started when we looked around us and found way, way more goblins. There were ten—no, more than twenty of them. Too many goblins!

"Let's scram!" We looked for an opening and started running, but the goblins growled and chased us relentlessly for killing some of their own.

We ran back the way we came. Brute and I were doing fine—we'd been running as a part of our training—but Lahtte and Horn were having a hard time keeping up now. At this rate, we wouldn't get away from the monsters.

Argh, what could we do? At this rate, we'd get too fatigued and they'd catch us. Over twenty goblins plus four equals bad. My brain went into high gear. Ms. Yuna's voice came into my head...

"If you wind up in a disadvantage during a fight, find a place that gives you the high ground. Even a little high ground is good."

And another time—what was it? "You're more than strong enough to beat goblins and wolves, as long as you fight them one at a time."

She'd told me we could fight in narrow pathways, on top of a bridge, or up in a tree with arrows and magic. Fighting safely was more important than being brave and dead. The only issue was that we didn't have the time to climb any trees when we were being chased. We didn't have any bridges or narrow pathways.

Unless we made one.

"We're heading this way."

"But Shin, that's the—"

"We can't get away at this rate. We gotta fight."

When we made it to the mountain, we turned our backs to it.

"We're fighting here. That way we won't have to watch our backs."

We would be cornered, but at least we wouldn't get attacked from behind. We wouldn't have to be afraid they'd come up behind us. As long as our backs were safe, we could focus on the fight ahead. Then we had to do what Ms. Yuna had told us: if the enemy had us outnumbered, all we had to do was take them down one at a time. We just had to create that situation.

"Horn! Can you make a wall?!"

Horn hadn't only learned how to go on the offense from Ms. Yuna—she'd learned how to make good use of earth magic too. "I can, but it'll fall apart right away with my magic."

"That's fine. Make a wall and guide the goblins' path."

Horn made the wall and did what I asked. When the goblins saw us, they would head right over instead of trying to break down the wall.

"Brute, you attack from the right, I'll take the left. Lahtte, you get them with arrows when you see an opening. Horn, you check your surroundings and maintain the wall."

They all nodded.

Somehow—*somehow*—it was over.

After we killed about fifteen of them, the other goblins ran off.

"Are we good?"

"Looks like we're good."

We collapsed onto the ground.

"I'm so impressed you even thought of that."

"I remembered what Ms. Yuna told me. She said that if we didn't have any chance of escape and had to fight, we've gotta flip the situation to our advantage as much as we can."

"Which is why you got us in a position with the mountain behind us and Horn's walls to the left and right."

"I saw Horn practicing those walls, so..." I knew that Horn had been mimicking Ms. Yuna's wall-making technique, but I also knew they weren't good enough for pure defense. "We were only safe because goblins aren't all that smart. We would've been in trouble if they broke down the walls."

I was glad I'd listened to what Ms. Yuna had taught me.

After catching our breath, we left and took a break in a safer spot. Then we headed back to the town, gave Ms. Helen our report, and were done with the quest. We hadn't been able to check the entire woods out, but we'd at least been able to report back that a goblin horde had probably formed.

They were going to start another survey soon, looked like.

We'd had a tough time with this quest, but once we got stronger, I wanted to be able to slay the more powerful monsters just like Ms. Yuna and Mr. Gil.

Noa Works at the Shop

WHILE I WAS HAVING LUNCH, Noa came into the Bear's Lounge. She noticed me right away.

"Are you eating as well, Yuna?"

"Do you mean you're about to join me?"

"Yes, I came to eat here too. It's been so long. May I?"

"Go for it."

"In that case, I'll order. Please wait for me."

Noa ordered some bread and cake, then came back.

"The bread this shop sells is so delicious."

"I appreciate it, Noa. Thank you." Noa ate her bread as she looked around the shop. Wondering what she could have been looking at, I followed her line of sight. She was watching the kids on the job.

"Yuna?"

"What is it?"

"I would also like to wear the bear clothes," Noa said, sounding quite serious as she watched the kids in their bear jackets.

"Uh...seriously? I mean, you're not joking?"

"I am serious. Fina and Shuri get to wear them. I'd like to as well."

Where did this come from? And what was I supposed to do about it? "Even if you want to wear it, it's still the shop uniform."

"Then do I need to work at the shop? I can do that. Now please, let me try on a jacket, won't you?" Noa put her hands together and begged me. Seeing that, I couldn't just tell her no anymore.

"Mil, hey, sorry. I know you're busy, but Noa says she has to wear one of the bear jackets and work." I'd called over Mil to fulfill Noa's wish, and we were at the changing room.

"Fine by me, as long as it's just for a short time."

"Thank you."

Mil seemed thrilled when I rested my hand on top of her head. Then I had Mil prepare a bear jacket. "Lady Noire, I did wash this, but...are you sure you want to wear my clothes?"

"I don't mind! That'll do just fine! Really, I mean it!"

"Are you sure?"

Mil seemed kind of put off by Noa's enthusiasm, but Noa undressed and changed into the bear jacket Mil had prepared her.

"Do you have a mirror?" she asked.

"We have one over there." They'd had a big mirror for a while to make sure they looked ready for work. Noa posed in front of it.

"Hee hee hee…I'm a bear! Grrr!"

"Noa," said Mil, "you're acting kind of scary."

"At last, I'm wearing the bear clothes!" Noa declared.

"Since you're wearing those clothes," I said, "we're going to put you to work."

"Yes, ma'am! Of course."

"And you can't fool around in the shop either. If you complain, it's over—got it?"

"I swear on the bear that I wouldn't dream of it!"

What was that supposed to mean? Was she swearing on herself now?

I decided to have Noa start with washing the dishes.

"Make sure you're doing it right."

"I've got it."

Noa didn't seem unwilling at all as she started to wash the dishes. When Morin saw that, she called me over, seeming worried.

"Yuna, are you sure you can put the lord's own daughter to work washing dishes?"

"That's what she wanted."

"Are you sure her father won't be upset later?"

"If he gets mad, I'll take the blame. Should be fine." Based on Cliff's personality, it wasn't like he'd storm into the shop or anything. If he got mad at anyone, it'd probably be Noa.

Noa didn't complain at all as she washed the built-up dishes.

"Yuna, I'm done! I want to bake the bread next. I made bear bread with Fina earlier."

"Hmm, how about we save the baking for next time?"

"Aww, but...but I've practiced!"

At that moment, Morin called over the kids in the kitchen. "If any of you are free, please peel some potatoes."

"Okaaay!"

One of the kids helping Morin answered back, picked up a knife with her tiny hand, then started to smoothly peel a potato. She was pretty practiced at it.

"Good job there."

"Thanks, Miss Yuna! I practiced really hard."

Noa immediately raised her hand. "I want to do it too!"

Morin blinked. "Noa?"

"I don't know," I said. "It'd be dangerous. She has to

use a knife and all..." If I let a noble get hurt, we'd have a problem on our hands.

"I'll be okay." But man, she was completely gung ho about it.

"Are you really sure?"

"Yes!"

Where did all that self-confidence she had come from? Now it was making me anxious.

Noa picked up the knife with her tiny hand and tried to peel a potato. It looked so dangerous, I just couldn't watch. Her knife slipped in a weird direction.

"Nope, no—" I took the knife from her "—you're going to hurt yourself!"

"Wh-what are you doing?!"

"Noa, no knives for you. No sharp objects." I couldn't let her use any—it just looked too dangerous. "This isn't your first time using a knife, is it?"

"Pssht. I've used knives, um...a couple...of times..." She mumbled that last part. I sighed. She was a girl from a high-class family. Guess that was just how things were. Fina and the orphans used knives all the time. Fina had learned the skill from butchering, and the orphans from cooking.

Noa forlornly set the potato on the table. I scratched my head and thought for a while.

"Noa, do it this way. Now watch carefully, okay? I'm not sure you'll really need to know how to do this, since you're an aristocrat, but..."

"That's not true at all. Please teach me."

I picked up the potato and knife, then slowly started showing her the proper way to peel it. It would've been nice to have a peeler, I'll admit, but the kids never needed them. Maybe it could make things go smoother, though...

Noa peeled the potato clumsily, but exactly like I'd shown her. "Uhh, this is hard..."

It was probably my imagination, but even the bear on her hood looked kind of bummed out.

After that, the three of us (me included) peeled the potatoes that Morin had asked for.

"I couldn't peel that many," she groaned.

"Everyone starts out as a beginner."

"Even you, Yuna?"

"Even me. Everybody." I consoled Noa, then we started moving toward the dining area after she asked for her next job.

"Am I serving customers next? Just leave it to me. I'll handle the money, pick up stuff, and wipe things down."

She did a turn, showing off her bear outfit.

Why was she so into this?

When I took Noa into the dining area, the kids were milling around doing their work with Karin at their center. Let's see...

"I guess we'll have you help out with picking things up? Um, hey, Karin!"

Karin was supervising as the lead on the floor. "Ms. Yuna, what is it? Oh, I feel like I've seen that girl somewhere before."

Noa pulled off her hood so her face was more visible. Her long blonde hair flowed out.

"Lady Noire?"

"Yep. She's helping out with the shop today in exchange for being able to wear the bear clothes."

"Uh, Yuna...are you sure? She's a noble..." Karin looked at me, then back at Noa.

"Well, she said she wanted to do this herself. I was thinking she could help clear the tables. If she gets in the way, just let me know."

"No way will I get in the way. I'll follow any direction you give me. Ms. Karin, what would you like me to do?"

"In...that case, could you clear the plates off the tables that customers have left? And wipe them down too, please."

"Do you know how to do that, Noa?"

"I've seen everyone else working, so I should be able to manage," Noa declared. And off she went to clean the tables, her little bear tail wagging from side to side.

"Ms. Yuna, are you really sure we should be doing this? No one is going to summon me about it later, right? I won't get in trouble for it?"

Karin sounded just like her mom.

"It'll be fine. I'll take all the responsibility for it."

Karin's worries aside, Noa's one day of work experience came to a close with nothing of note happening.

"I'm not paying you a wage for this, but we do have some pudding and bread if you want to take it home," I told her.

"Thank you." Noa accepted the bag and started to leave.

"Noa, wait one moment." I grabbed her shoulder.

"Wh-what is it? I need to head home soon."

"You can—after you've changed."

"Ugh, I thought I'd almost gotten away with it...and with the bear jacket."

She'd end up in trouble with Cliff and Lala if she went home dressed as a bear. She really seemed to forget her station sometimes. "C'mon, go change."

"You're so very mean, Yuna," Noa pouted.

She got changed back into her usual clothes—and

then tried to walk out the shop still holding the bear clothes in her hands. She really didn't know when to give up. Did she want a bear jacket that badly?

Though she didn't get to take the jacket home, Noa did look very pleased with herself when she left. Hmm. Maybe I'd better prepare a bear jacket for the next time she stopped by...

KUMA
KUMA
KUMA
BEAR

Afterword

THANK YOU for picking up Volume 7 of *Kuma Kuma Kuma Bear*. Time really has flown by. It's been two years since the first volume went on sale. Whenever I complete another volume, I wind up anxious it'll be the last, but we're just three volumes from breaking into double digits. That's my dream! And it's only possible because of everyone who's cheered me on. I never imagined this bear world would come so far.

At her core, Yuna is a girl who says she's doing things for herself, even though she's acting for the sake of others. In my mind, Yuna's fun brings happiness to those around her.

Volume 8 is planned for release before long. The bear world has plenty of stories left to tell, so I hope you'll come along for the ride!

In Volume 7, Yuna heads to the mines when she's asked by Ellelaura to take care of golems that have appeared there. However, she can't use her OP bear abilities in a cramped tunnel! If she overdoes it, the tunnel will collapse, and she'll cause a dreadful cave-in. Yuna digs deep, trying to find a solution, and manages to overcome the obstacles in her path.

Then—new to the books—Morin's relative Nerin makes an appearance. She's Morin's niece through her older brother. She was taken care of at Morin's house since she was little, when her father would have to travel for work. Since she grew up like that, she developed an interest in baking and made a pact with Morin to work at the bakery when she turned fifteen. Nerin ends up baking cakes at Yuna's shop and it flourishes even more than before.

I think Volume 8 might just have something to do with bear stuffed animals. Please look forward to it!

Finally, I'd like to thank everyone who worked to get this book out.

The illustrations, done in a legendary storybook style, were made by 029, who drew Yuna as the hero, Fina as the princess, and Ellelaura as the witch. Thank you so very much for fulfilling my requests and making them come true. I'm overwhelmed with gratitude.

I must thank my editor, whom I'm always causing trouble for because of my typos and omissions. And to all the many, many other people who were involved in the publishing *of Kuma Kuma Kuma Bear* Volume 7—thank you too!

I'm so grateful to the readers who've followed me this far. I hope we can meet again in Volume 8.

KUMANANO – ON A DAY IN JULY 2017

Experience these great light**novel** titles from Seven Seas Entertainment